A

Victim

in

Thug Mansion

Taboo

"A Victim in Thug Mansion"
- Taboo.
"Free Taboo Publishing LLC."
Copyright © 2024

ISBN: 978-1-963855-00-5

Also by this Author

A Victim of Justice

A Razor's Edge of Revenge

A Razor's Edge of Revenge Il

A Victim in Thug Mansion

A Hobbs Act Summer

A Razor's Edge of Revenge III

Non-Fiction Work:

A Message To My Teenage Self

Coming Soon:

The REAL Gangstas & Thugs of Palm Beach County

Preface

In no way does this author or Free Taboo Publishing, LLC. wish to glorify or promote gangs, drugs, or violence. Kids should take it as a warning, of what could happen, as well as what those consequences can be, and adults should teach the kids to avoid drugs, and gang activity, and to know the value of life. Do not throw your life away. All life is precious.

That being said, this book is a work of art, fiction, and meant to be entertainment. None of the people or names are real, nor are they intended to resemble anyone in real life. It does include real places to make it more real, as well as some real situations. It is FACTS that Congress has passed the First Step Act bill that takes the stacking out of the 924(c) stacking law, yet they consciously made the decision to allow all of those sentenced under this draconian law to stay imprisoned under this outdated and unfair sentencing enhancement. There are tens of thousands of people sentenced to hundreds of years, just like this author is currently sentenced to 91 years for non-violent, victimless drug and gun possession charges.

The current average federal sentence for murder is 22 years. This author was sentenced to over four times the national average federal murder sentence. Just for possession of things.

Not for anything violent. Not for any victims. Not for using the guns. He could have committed four murders and gotten less time.

Our sitting congress this year, 2022, has the SAFE Justice Act, the First Step Implementation Act, and many more bills for criminal justice reform just on hold in front of them. We need Congress to act NOW! Stop these unfair and ridiculous sentences! I encourage all of you who believe that the 851 and 924(c) laws are unfair to call or write to your Congressman and ask them to pass these bills! Ask for a change in this Criminal INjustice System!

TABOO

Dedication

This is dedicated to all those sex trafficking victims and any kid affected by the exploitation of their innocence. Sad to say, but you are survivors and what doesn't kill you only makes you stronger...

Acknowledgment

All thanks of course to my Lord Jesus Christ above all else. To my readers and fans who are in love with my work and support my dreams. A special thanks to Miss Ruth Okocha for all of her efforts towards editing this and all my books thus far and for putting them together so gracefully. Also, thanks to the graphic designer who does an amazing job! My mother Kathy Evans and Stepdad David Evans for raising my son to be a good person. To my Big Sister Laurie, for always being there for me. Mike Lee for riding this bid with me. Shane and Travis Stubblefield, my brothers from another mother.

Thanks to my family, Big Eric, EJ and Mikey. To Kira and Bella. Nichole Criss, Desiree Locke, Chad Lobsinger, Carmen and Mellissa Bezares. To Alyssa McCown and Jessica Mathis for all your support and help on this bid. To Jr, Kristi and Michelle "Momsdukes" Warner, Breanna and Pam Klein, Laura Webster (special), and Momo, Niki Hill, Craig Williams, Janel Abele, Heather Campbell, Tiffany, Tammy, Cassie Cabrera, Tasha Diaz, Zack Allen, Laura Mathis, Ivy, Rico, Lori and Athena Bailey. To Ena Weeks, Brandi Carter, Randy Abott, Budda, Cheryl Yeary, Jamie and Debbie Barrow, Natalie and Dina, Brat, Stephanie and Nicole Lewis, Lil Sherry Alane, Stephan and Livi Smith, Paulie, Samantha and all of the homies in the penitentiary on the front line:

To my friends and colleagues, MoneyRed and Sincere Echoes. To all the South homies! To da bottom- Tri-County area, 561: Money Mark, Revenue, Fats, Slime, Fee, Bankroll, Nasty, Biggs, BG, Al, Zoe, D, Herb, Nard, Razz, Roddy and 6th Street Willie...954-754: Chuck, Cheeks, Chance, Mal and Gutta...305-786: Snow, E, Big G, Smack, Iceman, Run-Run, JR, Lil Rob and the rest of Florida: Dizzy, Tay, Fruit, J-Ville, Bogie, JG(Big Homie), AP, Deek, Checkmate, Truly, Tank and O, its all love homies! Thank you all for the love and support to make this possible and all my other books, not just this one!

Thank you!

Prologue

alter idem (Latin): second self

November 1st. It is a cool night. Uncharacteristically cold for South Florida on the day after Halloween. The darkness was enveloping him. There were no street lights or dock lights at all, and of course that was by design. It was hard to be aware of a presence when you couldn't see your hand in front of your face.

Wicks is on the prowl. He is squatting his-over 6 foot, 190 pound frame-in the bushes of a concealed cut, opposite a small abandoned warehouse, on the west side of the Boynton Beach Inlet. "What is with me and ending up ducked off in some fucking bushes?" Wicks asks himself rhetorically. "You can't ask yourself a rhetorical question, it defeats the purpose of being rhetorical," said Jean. Wicks started at his alter ego's condescending remark, but he still smiled his 20 gold teeth, with his tattooed face, framed by his yellow dreads thicker than his wrist. Such a sarcastic smart ass.

Wicks knows he is getting worse with each passing day, but he couldn't say anything to any of his people or they might take it as a sign of weakness. He can't take that chance with all that he is on the verge of accomplishing. He had finally got a line on Lemonhead, and he couldn't risk any distractions. Not at a time like this. Lemonhead has to be dealt with immediately. Before he could escape again.

Lemonhead is a higher echelon expert importer in the Haitian Sensations drug cartel which tends to half of the South Florida drug supply. The only problem is: no agency, whether it be Federal or State, had ever been able to find anything on him or even uncover as much as his real name. Not that Wicks has ever dealt with any of these agencies. He works independently. He had already missed him once, when he had sent his homicide detective girlfriend and his Marine Sergeant nephew to take him out when their paths had crossed about a year ago, because he held Lemonhead personally responsible for his 11 year old nephew getting shot three times by a Haitian Sensations 14 year old prospect. Not only that, but a sharp influx on the presence of drugs and money at the local Youth Center where he and his girlfriend, Shelby, volunteered at, had also brought Lemonhead onto Wicks' shit list when he had uncovered how Lemonhead had ultimately been the one responsible for the kids having access to drugs.

Recently, they had found out that Lemon had been bringing in loads of foreign girls for the purposes of furthering his sex trafficking enterprise from Lil Haiti to Palm Beach County. He had also been trying to export American teenage sex workers and especially runaways, for his high paying politicians in the Caribbean Islands. Modern day slavery. Wicks couldn't stand it. He had to end this evil that existed in Lemonhead-and his enterprise-he had to be dealt with. Disposed of. No more, no less.

"What did you say? Repeat transmission please, Alpha ... " said Bravo, who is Wicks' Marine-turned-CIA nephew, EJ Morzella. And although nobody knew that EJ had started working with the Central Intelligence Agency, Wicks had been briefed in between the lines, the way that street niggas are known to communicate with each other.

"Nah, nothing, Bravo, still got nothing-wait, I'm seeing a vessel now. No running lights, looks like a cabin cruiser. This is it, Bravo-out," said Wicks, snapping out of what had almost certainly been a battle of personalities. Jean and Wicks are actually one person.

Wicks suffers from a mental neurosis called MPD, or Multiple Personality Disorder. Wicks was the controlling personality while faced with high stress or violent situations, and Jean Pierre, the alter ego, would be able to assume control under normal or non-violent circumstances, and under normal social conditions as well.

Having showed up on Shelby's black Yamaha R-1, Wicks put on his all black Kevlar motorcycle helmet, covering the tattoos on his face while giving him protection all the same. Hoping to be able to put in some work, he is dressed in all black clothes he has acquired from a Wal-Mart in Miami Gardens, down to his 'Jackboy' black Reebok Classics.

His nephew-EJ, is sitting on the rooftop of a condominium located across the intracoastal from their target location with his $20,000 Barrett M82 sniper rifle, to catch anyone by surprise who is posing a threat to their mission tonight. Being that EJ is now an asset with the CIA and can't be associated with any illegal activities, or even with operating on American soil, which goes against the interoffice policies of the Central Intelligence Agency, as well as the Department of Justice, he must keep his distance from the action.

§§§§

Shelby Nash, Wicks' live in girlfriend, has the dock wired for sound and is recording, so that they can hear the conversation of the players in the human trafficking and drug smuggling operation. She and Margarette were both present and watching from windows in the next door warehouse. Margarette is a victim that they had saved from Lemonhead when they had conducted the home invasion on his house, where she was being held as a sex slave for he and any of his associates that wanted to rape her. The warehouse is a fish packing house that smells horrible, but it provided the much needed cover for them to observe the arrival from. Margarette's presence was required because she had been the only one to ever bear witness to Lemonhead's face and was the only one who had the ability to identify him when he was expected to pop up for an appearance. She sat right next to Shelby with binoculars, as she was literally shaking with fear of seeing her tormentor again.

"Don't worry, Margarette. I'm here with you. It will all be over soon," said Shelby reassuringly, trying to ease her tension.

"I know. I'm okay, I just need to get this over with ... " replied Margarette, still shaking from the daunting task ahead of her.

Through the open warehouse window, they could hear the dual Mercruiser 350 small block engines coming from the cabin cruiser, a Wellcraft '32 St. Tropez, as it approached the nearby docks behind the warehouses. As soon as it landed, a dark-skinned black man with dreads like palm trees leaned forward and threw the lines to another figure who had just stepped out from the shadows of the dock, as the boat was just pulling up, obviously having been waiting for it to show.

"Detective Rodriguez, so nice of you to come and help us here. Is everything set for us to move the cargo?" asked a slightly accented voice, through the recording microphones out on the dock, set up for Shelby to hear.

"Everything is ready for you. I brought you a full size U-Haul truck and it's inside the warehouse. I don't want to know shit. Just give me my payment and I will follow you to give you safe passage to your Wellington jack shack, as always ... " replied the voice of the man the boater had identified as a police officer. A Detective Rodriguez.

§§§§

"Shit! Alpha, Bravo, fall back! Shit, this is a PBSO vice detective! I have to take him down myself, shit! I've always had a feeling ... shit ... " said Shelby into their makeshift COMS, or their communications system. The COMS they are using is simply their

13

own burner phones' bluetooth earpieces, connected by a merge-type of selection on their Galaxy S phones. Basically a three-way call, plus handsfree earpieces.

"Fuck no! Bravo, you stay fucking put and watch her back! Shelby, we can go together and I'll fall back once I know you're safe!" said Wicks, adamant in his dedication to her.

"Fuck! I don't have time to argue this shit! Alpha, do not engage law enforcement tango! I can never explain that cattle prod of yours away! Do not engage!" said Shelby, already moving from her position, frustrated and excited at the same time. She knew that she could not let Wicks engage in a gun battle with a law enforcement officer because of his stupid choice in a weapon system that he found so funny. But this wasn't some street hoodlums, where she could blame their deaths on gang violence and sweep it under the rug. This was a law enforcement officer, and there would have to be a full and thorough investigation where every stitch of evidence would be looked into. Her explanations would have to be accurate and thoroughly detailed, or she herself might find herself in some problems, and those, she definitely didn't need.

Wicks' choice of a weapon system that she was so pissed about was a Kel-Tec RDB Defender chambered in 5.56 mm, a NATO round, and he had a stick cattle prod attached to the length of the barrel. It was a futuristic and ridiculous looking piece of equipment and then, with a 50 round capacity extended magazine that hangs behind the pistol grip, almost like a part of the stock, in a banana clip styled magazine, it was definitely foreign looking, even thought it isn't. It's American. Wicks has always said that he had it so that he couldn't get a 922(g), or a Federal gun possession charge, as they had to prove that the gun travelled affecting interstate commerce, or basically that the gun had at one point in time, since its manufacture, travelled outside of its state or country of origin. The Kel-Tec hadn't. Kel-Tec is a gun company in Tampa, Florida. So, there could be no 922(g), possession by a convicted felon charge, reasoned Wicks, as he would smile with all 20 of his gold slugs shinning. Shelby just didn't have the heart to tell him that his ammunition for the gun did in fact travel interstate commerce, so it was still a 922(g) Federal gun case.

After telling Margarette to stay put, Shelby tightened the velcro straps on her Smith & Wesson level II bulletproof vest, and headed out with a Remington 870 Express Magnum Shotgun with a double pistol grip loaded with 12 gauge slugs, and her Sig Sauer P229 in her paddle holster. She was not surprised to find out this Detective Rodriguez was a dirty cop. She has always had a specific feeling about him because of the expensive clothes that he wore, as well as his fully restored 1978 Pontiac Firebird Ram Air. He had to have $100,000 into the whole restoration with the chromed-out engine, and it would be highly unlikely that he could afford all of that on a detective's salary, even in Palm Beach County where they had the highest payed Sheriffs Department in all of the whole United States.

Shelby Nash is an IAD Detective for Internal Affairs Division, and she had been taking down corrupt cops, prosecutors, lawyers and judges for over a year, since she has started at IAD. She had files on every suspected dirty vice cop in Palm Beach County, and Rodriguez wasn't one of them. This was a blessing that had fallen into her lap, and the fact that she had wired the docks and would have the admissions-and conversation with Lemonhead on record, was an extra bonus, and should be admissible in court. Or so she had thought.

She rounded the corner and couldn't believe what she was seeing. Detective Rodriguez was walking towards his car while figures in silhouetted forms on the boat were moving about, what she suspected were young girls, tied together by ropes around their necks. Shelby almost flipped out at the sight. Her heart ached, seeing in modern times, what looked like a slave ship unloading slaves. Her blood was boiling and she wasn't sure if Rodriguez would even make it to trial with the way she was currently feeling.

"Freeze-Rodriguez! IAD!" yelled Shelby, aggressively running up on the dirty cop as he was caught off guard by her violently aggressive and surprising attack. His face shook off the shock quickly and he tried to play his trump card, quickly adapting and trying to explain away his involvement.

"Okay-good, back-up is here! I was just about to bust this whole operation! Where is the rest of back-up?" asked Rodriguez, looking all around while trying to play it all off.

"Put your hands behind your head, fingers interlaced! Do it now!" shouts Shelby.

"Wha-what are you talking about? I'm Vice! I'm Detective Rodriguez, PBSO, and here to conduct a raid, why are you drawing your service pistol on me?" asked Rodriguez.

"I will not repeat my orders! It's all over, Rodriguez. Don't make shit harder on yourself than it has to be. Just give it up!" said Shelby, easing closer to him, ever so slightly, trying to make sure he doesn't try anything that will make things worse.

"Drop it, Miss Cop-Lady," said a voice as a Click-Clack of a slide being charged and a round being chambered from behind her could be heard. She can't see if it is a viable threat or not, but she knows that she is in a precarious position.

"If you fire, I'll take Rodriguez with me ... " said Shelby weakly.

"Two birds. One stone ... " said the voice simply, obviously not caring either way.

"What?! Wait! Now, come on, Rob. You guys can't do this without me! Now take it easy and let's all be reasonable," said Rodriguez desperately. "I'm sure this nice lady will be reasonable! Won't you? What's it going to cost to make you go away, Miss Lady?"

"You filthy piece of shit, there is no price in the world for my soul! Now, Rob, is it? You've got three seconds to put your gun down, or my sniper will spray half of you out to sea where you can

17

really become one with the Earth. One. Two. Thr-" Shelby started, but was interrupted.

A huge Boom from a distance away could be heard. The body that had just stood behind her flew almost five yards away, a full second before the Boom was even heard. Sonic Boom. A .50 caliber bullet fired from a Barrett sniper rifle was traveling at well past the speed of sound and could cut a body in half. An amazing piece of equipment. There was blood splatter everywhere. Shelby's back and Rodriguez's whole face had been sprayed. Shelby smiled in spite of herself. She had a lot of explaining to do, but at least she was alive, and at least it wasn't Wicks' stupid gun.

"AARRRG! Holy shit! What the fuck was that?!" screamed Rodriguez hysterically, spitting blood out of his mouth while looking wildly around as Shelby holstered her weapon, took out her cuffs and began cuffing him.

"That, my friend, is a .50 caliber tracer round. They'll blow ya back out, so don't make any kind of moves that will make my sniper nervous. That's not the type of feeling you want him to have on the other side of the scope. Now, come on ... " she said as she started to lead him away. She walked him all the way back to her unmarked motor pool car parked in the fish packing warehouse as she heard an automatic assault rifle shooting in three round bursts and another gun, a bigger caliber, possibly a .45 or a .50 caliber Desert Eagle, returning fire with big booms echoing in the silence of the cold dark night.

Another few big booms from the tracer rounds in the sniper rifle could be heard, and then there was just a still silence. Shelby knew she was in trouble with all of these unexplained shell casings of different weapons, but she hadn't even expected to stay in the area, or even to make arrests, but she couldn't un-ring that bell now. It had been her intention for this to be a hit, but it was an arrest of another corrupt cop. So, she decided that she would play it like it was a gang hit, while she had been there solely for Rodriguez being a corrupt pawn of these human traffic ring members. That was her only play. She just hadn't done any ground work on Rodriguez. No investigation on him whatsoever, and that could be a later problem for her.

"Alpha, Bravo, check in, and check out immediately. Get out of the area while I call this in ... "

She didn't even know if they had got Lemonhead or not, but taking down a corrupt cop like Rodriguez was worth tonight's activities. They freed some sex slaves in addition to his arrest though, so it was an eventful and successful night for all of them. They could get Lemonhead later. His luck would run out one day. They would get him. She is sure of that. Eventually, they would definitely get him ...

PART I

Six Months Late:

Celiane Jean

&

Sandino "Sweets" Armand

malis avibus (Latin):

under evil auspices

Chapter One

Celiane Jean is an incredibly smart and beautiful 15 year old girl. She goes to Lake Worth High School and is in the tenth grade. All of the boys, in and out of school, are always watching her. Seeing her walk, watching the way her hips sway in her jeans. Watching her in class, while she speaks-giving her reports, or reading her homework out loud, seeing her lips move and the way she forms her words. Some of the boys see a piece of moving art when they look at her, while others, see a pornographic prelude. An introduction of a sex goddess. They are infatuated, and yet, at the same time, they are scared to approach her, afraid of her daunting and intimidating being. But when Celiane looks at the boys in her high school, she really looks at the transparency of them, she sees them just as what they are, beyond all of the bravado and tough talk, just immature little boys, yet like dogs, she has to keep them away from humping her leg. Just like dogs, in fact. She knows they aren't much better. Simply stupid dogs trying to hunch.

Back when Celiane was a freshman, and was brand new to Lake Worth High School, and new to high school social policies in general, she had made a mistake. She got pimped. Or played. Used. Abused. Well, maybe not abused. But she had definitely been used. That was her mistake, and so now, she took an oath of abstinence, so it would never happen again. She would never be taken advantage of again. Not even if she was in love. She swore she would remain celibate, stay so until marriage. Her first high school experience had taught her as much, taught her that high school boys were just too immature. 'Childish' was an even better and more accurate description of them. She would never be made a fool of again. High school 101. She learned.

§§§§

Back about a year ago, Celiane had been seated in the row on the bleachers right behind the row of benches on which the players sat at their high school's third basketball game of the season at Lake Worth High School, when they played against their hated rivals, John I. Leonard High School. It was a big game as Lake Worth High School and John I. Leonard were more than mere rivals, they were enemies, from back when the school district rezoned an area south of Lake Worth to go to John I. Leonard High instead of Lake Worth High, where they usually attended.

The rivalry caused some problems with some of the local gangs as well. Some of the ball players from Lake Worth High got rezoned and were now playing against their good friends and team mates, who were also mad because it felt like their old friends and team mates were now traders, now playing for the enemy. Needless to say, there was tension so thick at the game that you could only be able to cut it with a chainsaw, and even that might not be strong enough to cut the tension. The crowds on one side of the gym had been specifically used by Lake Worth High School, and the other side, for the visiting team's families. But it was a big game and so crowded, so jam-packed with family, supporters and friends-that some folks were there seated on the opposite team's side, which in itself was causing a lot of additional drama. There was a lot of pent up aggression and anger in the gym. A lot of animosity. Even some hatred and evil intent. With all of the gasoline around, it could only take a spark to ignite.

Celiane, 14 at the time, had been scared, her heart racing and full of fear. They were packed in on either side of her, and she was being squeezed, pushed and shoved, back and forth between over-zealous fans. Polo had observed her directly behind him, saw her predicament, her unease, non-withstanding his watching his teammates play. Unexpectedly, he grabbed her hand to pull her out of the mix she was in. Out of the crowd and into his shining bubble of popularity.

"Sit here with me," Polo had said, smiling his perfect pearly whites that had instantly dazzled her. She was only 14 and boys had just began notice how wide her hips were, how thick her thighs are, and her budding breasts. She had all the physical attributes, but she was yet to have a real boyfriend. Little did she know that it was more because they were scared to ask her, than her being unattractive.

"Won't we get into trouble? I can't be allowed to sit here, right?" she asked.

"Who cares? If they want you to move, I'm going with ya! You're so pretty, baby girl! I go where you go," he answered, slick as oil, smiling pearly whites still demanding all of her attention and getting it too.

From that moment on, he had her. All the way deep into her bones, down to her soul, she was his. They began texting on their phones because Celiane wasn't allowed to have social media with her strict Haitian parents. Being Haitian in South Florida, and in Palm Beach County at that, was especially hard on Celiane. She had hardworking and honest parents. Morally decent, and church-going Christians, but a bit overbearing compared to all of Celiane's classmates and neighborhood friends. She didn't understand why her parents were so strict, so demanding. There were the unbearable rules to begin with. Demands. Curfews. Chores.

But then, the thing that Celiane hated the most, were her parents' insistence on choosing her friends for her. She had to either hang out with girls from her church, or if she would hang out with 'worldly friends', as her parents called them, her parents not only had to meet that friend, but also, that friend's parents, and invite them to their church, Grace Fellowship. That was usually enough to ensure that the potential 'friends' were no longer interested in being her friends. No girls that age wanted to go through all that, nor did they want to be be controlled. Then, there were the friends that ticked all her parents' boxes, however they were usually either indifferent or so boring, that

Celiane wouldn't even want to hang out with them anyway, or they were so outrageous in putting on a facade for the parents and were too crazy for her.

But not Polo, he had her. From the moment his big rough hands had grabbed her small soft one. She had never before felt so much attention being placed on her, and then, just like that, in front of almost two thousand people, he made her feel like she was the only one in the whole gym with him. He smiled and her heart fluttered and then melted. She couldn't even understand. What was it that he could like about her? Sure, she had filled out a lot just recently. She was a size 5-6 and had B-cups now. She guessed that she was okay looking in her face, she has full lips, a cute button nose, that is also wide and pretty. Long natural eyelashes and kinky hair that she kept either in a ponytail, or wavy to her shoulder blades. Nothing special that she saw. Yet Polo told her she was so pretty. He said she was prettier than even Lupita Nyong'o. He had even smiled when he said it. Said she looked so grown up. That she was sexy. She really hadn't even known what that meant at the time, but she had liked the way it sounded, liked the feeling, liked when he said it. That had been her downfall, she had believed and trusted him. The handsome white boy was giving her all of his attention.

His name was Mike Polowski, or 'Polo' to his friends. Even the coach and some of the teachers called him Polo. He had been a senior that year, and like a star. He was the star athlete, star student, and apparently, Celiane had not known, a well-known

25

star player. She found out too late. Their conversations together went well into the A.M on most nights, then there was texting all day, Snapchat and Facetime in between classes and practice. He had so many after school activities while she had to help with her little brothers, so they rarely got actual time alone. But eventually their phone sex turned into Facetime sex, which led to his pressing her to give him her virginity.

She relented. She did so because he had her. From the time he pulled her into his world, onto his bench during the game that night. She would have given him anything. She did give him anything. She gave him everything. She gave her innocence, her reputation, and her heart. What she had thought was her losing her virginity and them making sweet love in his bedroom while his parents were out, had actually all been a big setup. His webcam had been activated and was shooting the whole thing live, for all on the basketball team to watch and laugh. She had literally been just a bet. A bet that he had won. A bet that had destroyed Celiane and broke her delicate and immature heart, as well as her hymen, which was a very special thing to her.

The aftermath of it all had been devastating. When Celiane had tried to take her own life at school, jumping in front of a school bus after some students had streamed the sex tape on Porn Hub's amateur sex tape attraction, playing it in class for all to see, she failed. She had not only failed at her first, but surely not last attempt at suicide. She had failed her family. Failed her mama and papa, failed her *tonton* and little brothers. She failed her whole family and church. She could hear people's whispers as she passed by. She was now an embarrassment. A punchline. Used like how mothers scare their kids with Boogyman stories, they now scared the teenaged daughters with how 'if you kiss some boy, you will turn into a slut like Celiane, and everyone at school will laugh at you,' and the like.

Celiane didn't even blame them. Mothers had to use what weapons they had in their armory. Too bad for Celiane that she had become the grenade launcher. That, she didn't like. Couldn't accept.

§§§§

A year later, things were different now though, as she wasn't a naive little girl anymore. She wouldn't fall for a cute athlete's handsome smile again. A year older, at 15, she had persevered, she straightened her back and toughed through it. She was over the drama, over the laughs, and definitely over Polo. Now, she just completely ignored boys altogether. It would be safer that way. They weren't really even talking about what happened anymore, as most of those kids involved were seniors, so they had graduated and moved on. But she would never forget. She can't just forget it.

She now excelled more in school than ever before. She never again wanted to be seen just for her looks or to be a bet. She wanted to be respected and appreciated for her heart and mind as well. She wanted a man to love her, put her first before his friends or any other girl, and cherish her for her heart and for who she really is on the inside. The person she is. No high school boy could possibly do that, she surmised.

Celiane knew it was okay to be pretty, she couldn't help that, she even accepted it, although she did dress down a lot, covering herself more modestly. She never again wanted to be defined by her looks. She knew she was very intelligent, and she wanted it to always be a contributing factor to her description. She also knew that she had a really good heart, her brothers and parents told her that all the time. She was so good with her three little brothers, and she always took such good care of them while her parents were always working. She wanted that to be a contributing factor as well as her selflessness and her good heart. That was an important part of her. Of who she is.

Celiane had grown up on the South side of Lake Worth in the same house on E Street and 12th Avenue South that her parents have been renting for 17 years but would never be able to own. Her parents Michela and Josue had come from Port Au Prince, Haiti, 18 years ago after being invited by her uncle Michel, who was a member of the Haitian Sensations Organization. Michel had to pull some strings to get his favorite sister Michela over here. Michela is Michel's favorite sister for many reasons in her own right, but Michel always jokingly downplayed it by saying that she was his twin, so they were bound for life, like he couldn't get rid of her. In reality, he adores her, tolerates her husband, Josue, and absolutely doted on his niece and three nephews. He is always spending a good amount of his illegal earnings on them, especially since Michela was too proud of a woman to take handouts from her twin, even if they were as close as they actually were. She isn't that type of person to mooch off of her own family.

Celiane had a very special relationship with her uncle Michel, almost a father-daughter relationship, even though she already has a dad. For this reason, they were very careful that Michel was never told about the sex tape. Celiane loved her uncle and would die of embarrassment if he were to ever see or hear about that video. On top of the fact that she was ashamed, she also knew her uncle had recently been making a name for himself in the Haitian Sensations Cartel, and would try to retaliate on Polo and the kids who had posted the video on the PornHub website. She could not stand for her uncle to get into trouble because of her and the mess that she had created, she loved him too much to allow something like that to happen.

Celiane was just trying her best to move on with her life, get into a good college on an academic scholarship, so that her parents wouldn't be burdened by paying for her school tuition that she knew they would never be able to afford on their low income. It was for this reason that she had buckled down even more than she had the year before, when she had first gotten there to Lake Worth High School. A scholarship was more important than anything to her. She has so many hopes and dreams, as well as one day wanting to be the main provider for her family, as her parents had it hard, and she knew they deserved much better than they currently had it, taking care of her and her brothers on such a meager income despite working themselves to the bone.

Her father, Josue, is a machine shop technician. Or in real life terms, he would be called a mechanic. He worked at Grove Custom Auto, a machine shop in nearby Delray Beach that does rotors, valve jobs, surfacing heads, and even boring out engine blocks, among all of the other miscellaneous things they did there. Her father was happy in his simple family life and dead end job, although he didn't see past tomorrow for a future. There was no availability to ascend from his position. He would never have the money to start his own shop, and was unable to get a loan to start one for himself either. He has no medical or benefits, much less, a retirement plan. He was going to literally work till he died. Saw nothing wrong with that at all. It was just like any other life in Haiti, only here they were actually able to save money and make a better life for their kids. Although Josue would put on as if he was indifferent, he didn't just work so hard with no benefits just to survive. He and Michela saw past all of that 'living for today' American way of life. They both worked their fingers to the bone because they knew that they had to give their kids the best opportunities they could, and they knew they couldn't do so in Port Au Prince, or any other county other than America.

Michela works at Publix Supermarkets in the bakery, and has worked there for about 15 years. Not only did Publix give her benefits, but they sent her to a night school ESL or English Second Language class, so that she could learn to speak English perfectly, and eventually move up in the chain with the very family orientated company. Which she did, and would continue to do, because of her well-known work ethic. She worked so hard and was so pleasant, that they all loved and respected her. She was now the manager of the bakery, and would probably one day became a store manager, maybe even move up to corporate one day.

It was really Michela's job that kept the family afloat with all of her benefits and stocks in the Publix chain brand. Her English was just as prefect as that of her kids, to whom, English was a first language. She was a bright and happy woman who had grown up in controversial Port Au Prince, who had come far and made a better life for her family in South Florida. She was very grateful to have the opportunities she had made here. She was unapologetic to her poverty stricken remaining family in Haiti living in misery. She knew that life was all about some of the choices that we make. They had made theirs she had made hers, and now that the beds were made, they all had to accept and lay in them. She was very proud and happy to be in the position that she was in, and she had her brother, Michel to thank for that. She was grateful that he was able to get them over here to America and for them to have a better life.

Her only worry is, and always has been, her only daughter, Celiane. Maybe they had sheltered her a little too much. She was very naive, and in trying to blend in with her American friends, she has always been easily impressionable. She thought it would've gotten better after her suicide attempt and the whole sex tape thing, and in a way it did, but that was only on the surface. Michela knew her little girl and knew she was still very hurt and just playing it off for her mother's benefit. She was a romantic at heart, and therefore she would always allow her heart to yearn for what it most wanted, an everlasting and powerful love. She wanted-no-she needed to be swept off of her feet. She might act like she was over love, but she would never be over love, and that was what scared Michela, she is too much of a romantic and she glorifies her parents' own romance. But another situation like the Polo ordeal, and Celiane wouldn't be able to make it to college. She had an admirable and big heart, very selfless, but she was naive and impressionable enough to fall again in the same way that she had fallen for Polo. It was a scary thought. Something Michela would always worry about and stress to her husband, Josue, who would always reassure her that everything would be okay and work out for the best. It remains to be seen though.

§§§§

Celiane, Vera and Nicky, were coming out of the yoga and palates class that they took, over on 3rd Avenue North and Dixie

Highway on the Northside. Since none of them have a car, they walked across Dixie Highway in front of the little Guatemalan bodega and were going to begin their walk home. There was a group of guys a few years older than them surrounding a nice old school car in the parking lot that separated the bodega, from The Pegasus Restaurant that provided parking for them both.

Celiane was used to the cat calls and 'hey baby' shouts from the immature boy-dogs at school, but something different happened here on this night.

"PSSSSSST!"

Then a loud intake of breath could be heard, followed by: "PSSSSSST!" again, but even louder and more drawn out this time. Celiane was so pissed hearing this, she was tired of guys trying to "Psst" to her like she was a damn cat and had no feelings. Tired of the cat calls, 'hey babys', and just tired of ignorant little boys all together. This was exactly why she would never give another guy a chance! Men were all assholes, just like Polo and all of his little basketball friends and their bets.

"I'm so fucking sick of assholes like you doing that 'psst, psst' shit to get my attention! It's so fucking rude! We're not cats! 'Psst' don't work on-"

"Nah, sweetheart! You got me all wrong," said the handsome, mixed, almost red-complexioned guy with an amazingly bright smile and with eyes so beautiful that she thought that they could only be contacts. "I ain't cat callin' y'all!

33

Damn! It's my 'psst'-damn-tire's flat, 'psst', and I need your help, please ... " He then gave her his most illuminating smile of perfectly whitened pearls as he approached them even closer, walking towards the sidewalk that they were currently occupying, farther away and out of ear shot of the other guys that he had apparently been admiring the old school car with, until he was out all the way to the sidewalk. Next to them. Next to her.

Vera, her pretty Puerto Rican friend, and Nicky, her full-or plus-sized white friend, were already giggling from his attempt at humor. Whether he had planned it or not, Celiane was trying very hard not to give him the satisfaction of laughing because she knew that her thoughts were scrambled and then, out of nowhere, "You're trouble," busted out of her mouth, through the slight curve of the corners of her lips, giving up the hint of a small smile.

"No, sweetheart, I'm 'Sweets' and you already givin' me a toothache-sweet as you is ... "

Chapter Two

"Sweets" is a pimp. Not a pimp of the old days, like one of those real players in an Iceberg Slim or Donald Goines novel. Sweets was one of those that real pimps in those books would call a 'Chili Pimp' or even a 'gorilla pimp', from the way he was known to have put one bitch's head through the dry wall once. He worked no stroll. No Avenue. No corner. No strip either. This is 2024 after all, and Sweets considered himself to be a 'new age' pimp. And with the new age comes all of the perks as well. He did not refer to himself as a 'pimp' either. He called himself a 'Womanager', or basically, a man who manages women that provide services. Specialized services. Even escort services.

Starting out as a womanager, at first, he had run several ads that were on Backpage, and even Craigslist, but now, he does it a bit different, ever since the Federal Government had stepped down on those well-known websites. He now worked out of a base location at a 'jack shack', which is the common street term for the so-called massage parlors. The girls there basically pranced around in sexy lingerie and six inch high heels, and practically nothing else, and couldn't give a politically correct full body massage to save their lives. They do massage things though, and they are very talented at it, that was undeniable. A proven and well-known fact.

His Uncle Tree had started at this same shop 20 years ago,

pimping crackheads, and now, he owned this and two other jack shacks. He changed the name from Brooke's to 'Relax'. Then he made it where club membership was required. Tree had bought the place after the previous owners, a couple, were killed in a robbery. Now, he allowed his favorite nephew, and pimp-in-training, to have his own office to conduct his business, just as the previous owner, Noelle, had done for Tree, back when he was learning his trade as well.

Sweets wasn't interested in running a jack shack though. He stuck around for the free office, and to have a base where he could work the three girls that he did have when there were no out calls to go to. Without Backpage and Craigslist, Sweets worked his girls off of Onlyfans and Plenty of Fish pages. Sometimes he would use Tinder as well. That was because he had an underage girl that attracted a lot of older men, and what better place to offer her services than on Tinder? he had thought at the time when he had created those pages.

Sweets is still pretty young himself, at the age of 22, and he made sure to keep taking good care of himself. He was obsessed with it, in fact. Sweets is a very vain person. He loves his life and loves what he does for a living, his trade. Not many people get to get payed and make their living off of what they loved and were interested in, and that was his blessing: To be able to do what he loved and make a living at it. Sweets wants to live forever and do what he does forever. He wants to spoil himself. This is his only vice besides the occasional drink or two. He stays looking in the mirror. He is very handsome and knows it, some even say he is 'pretty', because of how he keeps himself so groomed. He also has so many skin creams and lotions, trying his hardest to preserve himself and looked like a typical college metrosexual pretty-boy. But Sweets is anything but feminine under all of the superficial outward appearances. He has a cold, calculating violent streak in him. A hard heart.

He is a very peculiar-blooded individual also. His father was Tree's big brother, and back in the day, they had been Black P-Stones in their native Chicago. That had lasted until the mid 90's when they had relocated to Florida with their stable of hoes to put on the stroll, Tree having just started learning at that time. Time had definitely changed since then. Their ancestral makeup was Nigerian and Armenian. Both sets of grandparents all had been immigrants as kids to Chicago via Ellis Island, New York back in the 1930's when the original Italian gangstas ran the Windy City. They had been honest people and did the best they could do with two grandsons, and four sons constantly drawn to the street life, a life they had chosen to reject after all they had achieved and the obstacles that they had overcome.

Sweets' paternal side being Nigerian and Armenian only added some color to his skin from his mother's pale Cuban side. His eyes were bright green, like his mother's, and when he smiles, he had perfect white teeth that he would never even consider crowning with gold slugs, no matter how popular the style in South Florida might be.

37

It should have only been inevitable that Sandino "Sweets" Armand would follow into this profession like his father before him, as he was very much the ladies' man. Not only were his features and Adonis-like, 6'2, 190 pound frame, attractive enough to be an actor and model, along with his golden-brown complexion, which made his bright green eyes stand out even more, but he was also blessed with the gift of gab. It is said that he cannot only 'talk a nun out her drawers', but he can also 'sell beach sand to a surfer'.

In school, he was known to tell one of two best friends that he loved only her and not her friend, and then vice versa, and carry on as long as six months in relationships with both of them, having them both keep the relationship a secret from the other for whatever random reason he could think up to give them. If he was ever caught, he would talk his way out of it and take them both to bed and carry on until he would find a new challenge, a new unobtainable girl that he would just have to have.

Right now, he has three girls in his stable already working, but he didn't feel the accomplishment that he should from having a three girl stable, even with the underage one, which is like gold to a womanager like him, as she is so very popular with the much older and rich men. She has some regulars, one of which is a Congressman and always did the dirty deed with her far East of the Bahamas, which is just a tad bit closer than Cuba is from Key West, where he can claim it was in 'International Waters', where he was under the impression that it wasn't illegal to have sex with a 15 year old girl. He was wrong about that, though. Tree and Sweets had laughed out loud a whole lot on that one. An idiot Congressman who wrote and passed laws, but didn't even know when he himself was breaking them. That is one of the main reasons that Congress, and in turn, the whole country, is so messed up and backwards now.

But, overall, Sweets is a people person, charismatic and convincing in his complicated facade as well. People generally did what he asked of them, because in doing so, it made them feel like a part of his world and got his attention. If you knew Sweets, his attention was definitely something that he made sure you wanted to get. That was by design. Not only had he read all of the Robert Greene books, from "*The Art of Seduction*", all the way to "*48 Laws of Power*" and studied them as if his life depended on it. He also had taken a starting two year course at PBCC or Palm Beach Community College, for psychology, and even dated his psych teacher for one of those two years. He had learned more from her in one year as a woman than he had from two years of being in her classes as a student. She still always called him. She made it obvious that she was the one that hadn't learned.

Life working out of Relax, the jack shack wasn't all that bad though. Men would come in the front door after being buzzed in when they showed their current membership card, or after they initiated the paperwork for the new membership, an initiation process where their backgrounds were completely vetted. The first sight they would see would be all of the available girls, any girls who were currently not renting a room. All dressed up in cute little negligee, teddies, lingerie-or in some cases, they would be completely naked, depending on their own preferences. There he would choose a certain girl, or girls, that he would get a timed session with. Sessions varied in which room or time period the member might choose, which would contribute to the determination of what that session price would turn out to be.

Generally, 30 minute sessions were $300, one hour sessions, $500. In either case, the facilitator was to be 'tipped' whatever the amount that the room fee was. One hour sessions would cost the member $1,000 total. Half for the room fee, and half for her tip. Nothing is negotiable. This is all based upon there being no penetration. Facilitators could work out their own deal once in the room with the member, if it involved penetration or any other fetishes, that was at the facilitators' discretion, of course. As long as Tree's bank account at the end of the night, matched the girls' time in the rooms, and the girls were taken care of, he didn't care about what went on in the rooms. He had signs posted up everywhere around about how prostitution was strictly prohibited and how Relax cannot be responsible for what the girls do behind closed doors. Disclaimers. Signs to keep Tree from being arrested for running a prostitution house and facing pandering charges. Disclaimers that contradicted everything that was actually going on inside and behind the closed doors of Relax.

Of course the girls always would talk, sharing secrets and laughing at members' fetishes. There had been the guy who would lick Brat's feet and then climax, spilling his seed all in between her toes. The guy that payed for April to kick him in his balls repeatedly from different angles, as he would cry to himself awaiting the next ball busting kick. One guy payed Lisa to just walk around in panties and high heels while he continually smoked crack and tried his very best to ignore her.

All the while, Sweets could watch on the camera monitors hidden in a hall closet, laughing at the content gained from cameras that weren't even supposed to be there. It was more than just for kicks to Sweets though, he actually learned from the customers, and from all of their eccentricities and fetishes. He would really learn from their human nature. You could never understand a woman until you first understood their motivation. Men motivate them in one way or another. If it be a money transaction with a john or a move she makes for her pimp. Either way, Sweets had figured that behind every bad bitch, there is a man who motivated her, one who could simply ask her to do something for him. Something, that ultimately, helped to benefit them. Whether she had sex with him, or did it with a stranger for him, she was motivated to please him. The man who motivated her.

Sweets had motivated many girls, but he had never found the one that could bank roll his next level plans. He wanted to own his own strip club with a massage parlor inside or attached to it. He wanted to be a legally recognized womanager and be one of the only pimps in the game to build a massage-strip club. Want a lap dance? Ok, cool. Want a massage too? Massages are 5 songs minimum, lap dances 2 songs. Fuck the Players Ball, Sweets is a new age pimp. He wanted to make it happen and had even researched about how to go about it too. Liquor licenses go for about $300,000 in South Florida because they weren't issued to the public anymore. You had to really want it because you had to pay to buy it from a current club owner who was shutting down. The way the club scene in South Florida is, there was not much chance of that happening. It would be very unlikely. So, he would use his uncle's influence to make it happen.

The other part of his dream was that he wanted to build this all on the back of one bad ass bitch. He wanted to build his empire, his dreams, off of hoe money. In that way, he is a pimp, one of the olds. He wasn't just in it for the present. He saw and wanted to build a future. Wanted something big and everlasting. He wanted his girls to share in his vision and want to chase the same dream as well, and he knew with his current stable, or his team of girls, they weren't enough to fulfill his vision with. He needed more.

He really needed a game changer. He needed a super-hoe. One he could train, shape and mold into something special. One who could not only envision his dreams with him, but someone who could actively participate in and help build those dreams into a reality. A hoe who would be able to help him realize his dreams, and then once achieved, could enjoy life with him, living the same dreams with him. He wanted what every man basically wanted: A

42

hoe to share the rest of his life with. But first he would have to find her, then he would have to use her to build his empire. It would not be an easy task, or a pretty one, but Sweets knew he had it in his blood. Pimping and womanagering, were what Sweets would live and die by. Pimpology, the only Ph.D he would ever be needing in his life.

"Nayla! Get your shit together! Lets's go!" said Sweets, trying to rush his youngest girl into hurrying up. She always took forever to get ready.

"Okay, daddy, I'm comin', damn ... " said Nayla, a beautiful, yet very underage Cuban girl. At 16 she looks at least 25, except for her young and pretty face.

Sofia and Angel were both already seated in his dunk, a '73 Chevy Impala convertible. So beautiful is his car, that he named her 'Bella', which means beautiful in Italian. It is candy painted money green to match his appetite, as well as his eyes, with white soft leather interior and white Giovanna rims to match his teeth. The "28's had his Bella sitting up high in the air and made everyone around, pay Bella, and in turn, Sweets, their attention and respect. She would beat the old pimp Cadillacs back in the day in every way imaginable. She is a complete masterpiece.

Having a beautiful ride like Bella, he always wanted to make sure that he had beautiful cargo to match. Hence, Sofia, Angel, and Nayla. Sofia is Puerto Rican, 5'2 and about 110lbs soaking wet. She has curly long hair down to her small cute little butt, tanned skin and a pretty face. At 22, she had already been selling pussy for five years for Sweets, who was the the original one who had turned her out, and with whom she had been in love with since high school.

Angel, on the other hand, has dark skin and is 5'6, 150 pounds, a nice and plump apple bottom ass, big boobs-some D-cups-and big thick legs. She was the most popular at Cheetah's Palm Beach, a gentleman's club that is anything but gentle, for poppin' and twerkin' her ass on the stripper poles. Sweets occasionally would take the girls to Cheetah's to make extra money on slow nights, when he could leave Nayla alone at Relax to work by herself. She was so young and new, so he would always watch the tapes of her later on, and keep track of his money, as well as her progress.

Sweets knew that Sofia was special because he had pulled her all on his own and turned her out, or convinced her to trick for him. But Angel and young Nayla had been tricking for Wild Bill. Sweets and Wild Bill had gotten into an argument one day that had turned into some gangsta shit, and Wild Bill was missing ever since. No face-no case.. Therefore, in accordance with South Florida street code, Sweets is now responsible for taking care of Angel and Nayla, who are still great additions to his growing stable. The fact that Wild Bill was such a seasoned vet, and had trained Angel and Nayla well, was also what helped Sweets in his own game. Sweets was learning a lot from them, and the extensive training that Wild Bill had given them, and so he was very grateful to have them on his team. Well, except for when Nayla was never ready to go on time, and that alone drives him crazy. "Perfection takes time," she would always say. That would really piss him off a lot too since she could literally just start preparing herself earlier and be ready on time, instead of starting late and being late all the time. Another con of having to do all the thinking for the girls.

Nayla finally jumped into the backseat with Angel, as Sofia was already used to always sitting shotgun and Sweets could think of no reason to change it when Angel and Nayla joined his stable. Sweets smiled as he slid on his Gucci shades, turned up Kodak Black's '*Haitian Boy Kodak*' album to make the four Memphis Mojo "15's in his trunk start beating up the trunk lid, and he pulled off, confident about how great life was. How much greater it would be when he finally found his Hoe-Mate, which is a pimp's soulmate. The one on which he will build his empire and spend the rest of the great life with. It is his destiny to be the best of that. He and everyone who knows him is sure of.

Chapter Three

Celiane, Vera, and Nicky walked to Lake Worth Beach from Vera's apartment, which is next to Bryant Park, or just across the Lake Worth bridge, maybe about a 5 minute walk from the beach. Celiane and Nicky always loved staying over at Vera's house. Vera's parents were Christians and went to church and all, but they weren't unnecessarily overbearing, as Celiane's parents are, or even absent, like Nicky's. Vera's mom would check on them once in a while, but she wasn't ever going to be the hovering "Helicopter Mom" type. Sometimes, she would even drop them off and pick them up all the way out west at Wellington Mall, and that is a 15 minute drive each way. Celiane knows something like that would be completely out of the question with her strict parents. Michela might one day take Celiane to the mall or something, but to leave her there unattended? Impossible. She was always so sheltered, so controlled. One day, she had gone with a friend to get her dog from the pound and saw them all in those inhumane cages, she remembered feeling a kind of kinship with those animals. She resents her own imprisonment actually, and she feels that it condescended her. Made her feel like she was trapped and couldn't be trusted to make her own decisions. To live her own life. Like she wasn't almost grown.

When they got to Lake Worth Beach, before they were even hit by the sun and sand, they were all hungry, so they decided to go to Lake Worth Pizza, a pizza parlor that is located on what is known as 'The Strip'. The strip is a strip plaza that runs parallel to the beach and the water. It hosts a public pool, gift shop, surf shop, pizza shop, and a few other small businesses, as well as the big casino, which is now a big attraction that provides a venue for big weddings, and other such big events that were important or political, in addition to the safe gambling venue that it is.

While seated on the outside patio of the pizza shop, eating their single slices of cheese pizza, they small-talked and watched the show cars all pass on the strip, which basically went in a big circle around the pool, plaza, and big parking lot, and came around again with turn off options to either go back to the city of Lake Worth, continue along the beach on A1A, North or South, or come back around for another pass at the strip.

"Vera, so what's up with you and T-Zoe?" asked Nicky, forever being nosey.

"Shit, he got me this cute little chain with a heart that says ... you see?" asked Vera, who is a very beautiful, tan-skinned girl about 5'3 and 120 pounds with curly hair and a pretty face, showing them her necklace. The heart-shaped medallion said 'Puerto Rican Princess' all in yellow gold and a few diamond chips to make it stand out a little more, even if it wasn't the most expensive gift. At 16, Vera and her boyfriend, T-Zoe, were in a very serious relationship, as well as sexually active and had just had their first anniversary. Both were 100% committed to each other and it was definitely a relationship that Nicky and Celiane envied. It was the type of relationship Celiane should have had with Polo, but had instead got played and hurt.

"Girl, it's beautiful. That boy sho' do love you," said Celiane, envious and yet still happy for her good friend.

"Yea, Vera, that's nice! What did you get him for your anniversary?" asked Nicky.

"Girl, you do not wanna know! You know that thing he always wantin' me to do. That nasty shit he always askin' for, well I looked that shit up on Porn Hub ... and girl, I did that. And I ain't even gon' lie, that shit was sooo good! Wow! We definitely doin' that shit from now on! Girl, he is that nigga, for sure!" answered Vera, grateful to have her man.

"Girl, you is so damn nasty! You did not do that!" said Nicky, as she secretly wished it was her that he was with, always the envious one.

"Damn right, I did. And going to keep doing it too!" retorted Vera laughing.

"T-M-I, girl! And by the way, gross, eeww. .. " said Celiane, also wishing it was her.

"Yea, whatever, girl. What about you and Mr. Triple A with the flat tires, just 'psssting' away? Think I ain't peep that look that passed between you two?"

"Anyways, I am not thinking about no boys right now, I don't need no boy humping my leg, all horny and shit, like a damn dog! I'm good, thank you very much!" replied Celiane.

"Girl, you is always talking about that damn 'dogs humping

legs' shit, girl, you starting to make me wonder!" They all started laughing before Vera continued, "And are you forgetting that we saw him too, and that man was no 'boy', that was a man, and with his pretty green-eyed self, you lucky I got T-Zoe or I might have had to relieve you of his sexy ass! Damn he was fine! And payed too, by the look of those Balmains and Christian Louboutin shoes. Girl, you need to get your head out your ass. We all seen he was feelin' you too, girl. Just sayin'."

"Girl, N-E-ways, he liked what he saw, he don't know me to be even starting to feel me like that, that's all that sweet talk shit, any-way-girl-bye!" said Celiane with finality in her face and tone, attempting to end the discussion.

"Uh-huh, girl. Just sayin'," said Nicky, their plus-sized white friend, who was always thirsty, and always lived her life through the lives of her friends. Nicky is the oldest of their little crew. At 17, she was more experienced and popular with the boys with her sexual willingness, yet would never be as well liked as Celiane and Vera, as their personalities were so deep, while she was a very shallow and simple person, all about the physicalities and nothing further than skin-deep.

"Just sayin' what, Nicky? You dig him so much, then you holla at him, okay?" said Celiane, getting frustrated.

"Okay, well damn. . . Maybe I will, " said Nicky, and they left the subject alone, knowing that when Celiane was ready to talk, she would. They wouldn't push. Well, they wouldn't push anymore today, but they both, never minding Nicky's thirstiness, wanted Celiane to be happy again. Not so serious all the time. They both wanted their pre-sextape friend back. So, push they might. Just not anymore today.

Once the girls finished their slices, they walked down the strip towards the pier on the beach side. Lake Worth's beach is second only to the likes of the Florida Keys' clear, aqua-blue beautiful waters. Its waves are not too big, and you could see almost ten feet to the bottom clearly, beautiful fish and sea. Celiane always loved to walk the pier in order to see the bottom from so high up. It always reminds her that there is a God, and that he loves her enough to allow her to see such perfection in this beauty.

"Let's find a spot to post up at, " said Vera, as she always does, ready to set up their beach towels and show off her beautifully tanned skin and bikini body.

"I'ma go hit the pier, y'all go on ahead," said Celiane, as she always does, to have a few moments to herself and appreciate the beauty of the amazing Atlantic Ocean and its marvelous fish that could be observed from above the pier.

"Okay, but don't be all day up there! You always leavin' us, goin' up there to smell those nasty fish!" said Nicky, commenting on the fish smell because there are so many people fishing up there, hence the pungent smell of dead fish.

"Okay, I won't be long, don't trip ... " said Celiane, walking away.

Vera and Nicky looked at each other, shrugged, turned and walked into the beach sand. Being friends with Celiane for years since middle school had obviously gotten them used to her eccentricities as well as her mood swings. She could be sometimes as deep as the ocean, and yet other times, her needs so simple. It was hard to read Celiane ever since the sex tape incident, and being her friends, neither gave them any understanding-nor any insight-into her ocean of feelings and emotions. They agreed that it was best to just give their friend some space sometimes and leave her to her own devices.

Celiane walked along the north side of the pier, where there is an ice-cream shop, and as she passed it, she decided to get an ice-cream cone to eat along her walk on the pier. She got a cookie dough chunk ice-cream with sprinkles and a cherry topping and began her walk towards the end of the pier, trying to see some of those beautiful fish over the side of the railings. She was always so captivated by all of the underwater beauty, knowing that there is a whole other world living under the water. She absolutely loved the starfish. She recognizes that they were another example of God's amazing creativity and design. She thought she spotted one as she neared the very end of the pier, so she tried to get a better view. Without looking, she bumped into someone.

"Oh, excuse me, I-" She looked up as she was apologizing and saw, it was him. The pretty green-eyed boy, or man, from the parking lot at the bodega that she had met a few nights ago. He had made her friends laugh with his flat tire joke. She froze up.

"I can see my destiny is here ... " he said, and smiled those perfect pearly teeth.

"You're-huh? What?" Celiane asked, flustered, not quite sure she was understanding him correctly. He has thrown her for a loop.

"I mean it's got to be destiny, right? First I see you and then now, you just literally bumped into me. Maybe it's fate." His smile was so frustrating to her, yet infectious. It was almost impossible for her to look away, but she mustn't let on about it. She can't ever let him know of the effect that he was having on her.

"I-I was just looking at fish," she said and then noticed the binoculars hanging from a strap around his neck, "I guess with those binoculars, you are checking out for girls out there going sunbathing? How incredibly cliche-"

"I love the ships. Way out there," he pointed gently, interrupting her, then offered her the binoculars. Surprising herself, Celiane accepted them from his well manicured, offering hand. She placed them up to her eyes and searched. She saw what he meant. Miles east of them, close to the Bahamas.

"Beautiful, aren't they?" he asked. "Coming and going on important missions. There's a Navy ship to the left, a tanker straight ahead, and that is a 15 floor cruise ship, over to the right, heading to the Port of Miami. You can even zoom in and look at all the people on the deck." He smiled again. A sincere smile. 'Trouble', she thought to herself knowingly.

"And you were looking out here and not back at the beach girls getting their tan? You expect me to believe that?" asked Celiane, laughing out loud.

"Hey! I'm not a perv or nothing, okay? I'm 'Sweets'." He held out his hand, waiting for her to take it.

Chapter Four

Sweets is driving his dunk, Bella, on the strip at Lake Worth Beach. He would tell the girls every Sunday that he was taking them to the beach for some fun in the sun, for them to enjoy the fruits of their labor, by being seen in Bella, having fun, and getting some sun. But his ulterior motives, and as a womanager, there were always ulterior motives, was for him to not only find new clients, but to knock-or to pull someone else's bitch-new girls, and to put some sun on his girls' skin to keep them healthy and looking good. Them having fun and enjoying themselves was always an unnecessary byproduct, and it was usually short-lived anyway, as he almost always found a new John, or client for them to pleasure in the public restroom, underneath the pier, or for the voyeuristic, in the beach water in front of hundreds of unsuspecting beach goers. Half of whom were most likely doing the same thing in the water.

He lets his girls go enjoy themselves, after parking Bella in the no parking zone, directly in front of the Lake Worth Pier's bar, where she would gather the most attention from passerbys. He gave the bartender, Ena, a $100 bill, so she would move Bella if twelve came around looking, and Ena gave him a Heineken for him to sip on while he took her binoculars and walked along the Lake Worth Pier, searching for new talent or clients, whichever he could come across, on this South Florida sunny pre-summer day.

54

He didn't see anything too interesting as he passed the pier's restaurant, which was where, underneath the pier, the water line began in its lowest tide. So, he decided to walk to the end of the pier, where all the fishermen were. At least he could look at the ships he loved to see while he allowed his mind to wonder. This was actually the only time he could get away from his girls and do some real damn thinking. They were always talking. They just never shut up. He would think that they would want some moments to themselves, but they never gave him space. He could never get a moment or some time to himself when they were around him. It annoyed him to no end, but he also respected the fact that as a womanager, he had to play his part, just as they must always play theirs.

Standing there contemplating, while leaning against the pier's railing was where he was when the beautiful little Haitian girl literally bumped into him. She was a godsend, and there was no possible way that bumping into her again was some kind of coincidence. Life was just too good for that. But he said the first thing that came to his mind anyway. Some random shit about destiny. He already had forgotten as he appraised how damn bad the girl actually was.

Celiane is her name, he remembered. About 5'7, 150 pounds, with a round perfect bubble butt, C-cup breasts, perfect lips and smile. A cute little pert nose and amazing eyes. This was a girl he could put in magazines, better yet, in movies. The best thing yet, was that she didn't even know. A body like this and she wears a

55

one piece bathing suit? She dresses down, and for what? This was a girl that Sweets knew he could work with. He was an expert working with her type. This is his business, his chosen profession. A womanager. She needed him, he needed her.

She is self-conscious. He could see that much right off. Low self-esteem, she didn't know how beautiful she is or how damn fine her body is. He can definitely use that. He wouldn't need to tear her down before building her up as he always had with the others. She was already as low as she needed to be, and he can do magic with where she was in her self-image. He just needed a con. A way to get over or through the wall she had built to protect herself. She had been hurt. He can tell, and it had been bad. Again, tools that he could use and work with. He needed an 'in'. Without a way in, he would never get her to open up, never get past that wall she had built up for protection.

Whatever it had been that she went through, it had been terrifying for her. One of his gifts that was instilled inside of his blood is reading people, and in reading her, the downplaying her own body; the protective wall built around her heart; all taken together with her quick retorts, he noticed that she had wanted to laugh with her friends when he had made his joke on the first night they had met, but that she wouldn't allow herself to do so. She didn't want anyone to start trying to know her, couldn't allow herself to open that door, didn't want a chance at being hurt again. He knew that she would hurt though, once he breaks her, she will hurt like never before. They always do when he breaks them, it's

56

just a part of the process. His process.

She really didn't give him an opening. She was standoffish as he had suspected that she would be. It merely confirmed his reading of her. She was a closed book, but one that he needed to open and conquer. Read, memorize, and then rewrite in his own hand. In his style of writing. He was going to have to stretch this out all the way. Baby steps. He would have to use that old psychology technique, the taking of baby steps with everything and anything in relation to her progress. Breaking the ice was only the first baby step, and he was only about a quarter of the way at that. This was going to be an enormous challenge, but the rewards, he knew, would far outweigh the work.

"So, if you ain't come to check out the ships, what are you ... ?" he asked, feigning confusion and trailing off in the rest of his thought.

"I sometimes use this place to think, clear my head, and ... well, I like to see the ocean floor and the fish down there. They always come around the pier for some reason."

"Yea, they are beautiful, and it's very tranquil up here, I can see how being here could clear your head. Now I feel stupid for watching those ships with so much beauty right underneath ... and right here," he said, staring into her eyes. She seemed to accept this, then added, taking her eyes away from his momentarily, "Well, underneath anyway."

"Don't you appreciate the beauty topside as well?" he asked

her, trying to read every tell he could off of her, anything that he could later use in this psychological battle of the wits. Her, trying to keep him out; Him, trying everything he could, anything for him to get through her incredibly thick and solid wall.

"I suppose, except that almost everything is beautiful and amazing from a long distance. Like your ships. Like the Sun. But ships can sink and the Sun will burn if you get too close or even if you stare at it for too long."

"Yea, but I wasn't referring to things in the distance. I was referring to beauty right in front of me. Are you saying the beauty in front of me will sink my ship, or even burn my eyes if I stare too long at it? So, you're really saying that your beauty is dangerous?" he asked her, smiling deeply, contemplating.

"No," she said, as she put her soft hand on his chest, forging a barrier and pushing him away as she began walking away from him. "I was referring to yours. I'm sorry, but I have to go. Enjoy your ships."

With that said, she continued walking away from him, leaving him with his own thoughts and his mouth hanging open. He was completely flabbergasted. Did he just get played? Did she just reject him? he asks himself.

Hold up, he thought to himself, sitting there and watching her hips sway and move, as she left him there with his mouth agape, did that just really happen, she turned and left him there? He replayed the whole conversation again in his mind. Sure enough, she downplayed her own beauty, exalted his own, and yet, she still left him sitting here, and consciously made a decision to leave without giving him her number. It was completely unheard of. It sure as hell had never happened to him before, because when he met girls they always wanted him more than he wanted them. But not, or so it seemed, with this beautiful Haitian girl. Now he was curious, to say the least.

He would have to take baby steps. But how could he take baby steps with no number? No Facebook, no Instagram, no smoke signals, nothing? Shit, he barely got her name. There were some hints of information he did have. It was something that he could work with when he really thought about it. He met her once on a Friday, coming out of the yoga studio and then she bumped into him on a Sunday at Lake Worth Pier. These were the things that he needed to remember if he was to orchestrate another chance meeting, in which he can continue to use his baby step technique to wear down that big ass wall that she has up around her. But he would definitely wear it down eventually. Plus, he doesn't give up easy.

This is the first time that a girl didn't even have to give him a number to put him to work, how did she think he would find her with no phone number to call. That was the main point though, he realized, she didn't. She was really that closed, that she didn't even consider him an option.

He was thrown for a loop, but he knew that with time he would pull her, and then he would turn her out and they would build an empire together. With his brains and her beauty, he knew there was no limit to what they could accomplish. He would have to work hard, earn her trust and love, and then use it to get her going like he knew she could be. A million dollar pussy, he could just feel her potential.

He watched her walk away with the binoculars and saw her go to the beach, meet and join the same friends that he had met her with on that first Friday night, coming out of the Guatemalan bodega. She hadn't mentioned them, thus, just as he suspected, she was going to take so many baby steps, she was a challenge, and he liked and appreciated a challenge, any day of the week.

Sweets walked back out front and went looking for his girls. He would have to be careful with them. He couldn't risk blowing his chances with Miss Celiane before he even got started. She would definitely shut down if she discovered that he already has three girls, and that he was also a womanager, well finds out the meaning of 'womanager'. He would take no risk with her, she was the one. She could take his plans to the next level and he knew it. She was the one for sure. Baby steps, he tells himself, baby steps. 'Patience is a virtue' is the saying, and he would use that to develop his, into some baby steps for her.

Chapter Five

Celiane's week, after the second meeting with the green-eyed-silver-tongued devil, as she thought of him, went pretty much as any other normal week. She helped with her little brothers while her parents worked, went to school, ignoring the boy-dogs, did her homework, studied, and talked to Vera on the phone, since she was rarely allowed out on weeknights. Occasionally, she would attend the youth group at the Grace Fellowship Church. She only did so in order to get out of the house, though. She really loves her family-her brothers-but sometimes it was a bit too much of a responsibility to bear, she wanted a little bit of freedom and just couldn't understand why all of the other girls her age would be able to go hang out, go to the Youth Center, the mall, friends' houses, or the bowling alley, and she was always expected inside before the streetlights came on. She felt even more pre-pubescent than a teenager.

For the last year or so, Celiane had taken a liking to taking midnight walks through the neighborhood to clear her head when she couldn't sleep, she would sneak out after her parents had fallen asleep. She usually wore a jacket with a hoodie and sweatpants, but it was summer now, so she had to cut that down, the South Florida weather being as hot as it currently was. Still, this late at night walking the mean streets of Lake Worth, she had to be careful. Lake Worth was the city known for "The newly weds and nearly deads", so she wears a hat and some baggy clothes to disguise her body. Having herself get recognized would be an even worse fate than being harassed by some street scum, because if her parents found out about her middle of the night walks, they were sure to put bars on her windows, and then she would really feel incarcerated and be in trouble. She couldn't lose this little slice of heaven-this small feeling of freedom that she felt when she would be alone on her walks. These peaceful and tranquil walks meant everything to her, and as long as she minded her business, kept her eyes focused straight ahead and avoided the hoodlums, they usually wouldn't bother her either.

Her mind wondered all over during her walks. Nothing was off limits, and even though she tried not to, sometimes, she would even think about Polo. About what he did. Also, about what he didn't do. Sure, he had caused the whole thing in a way, a very big way really, but the tape getting out had never been his doing and he had messaged her and begged profusely, apologizing continually.

That was all before the investigation of course, when she had tried to kill herself and the school safety officer had wanted to know why. That was when it had all finally come out. The truth. Charges had been filed and Sharod Bell had been arrested for posting underage porn on the PornHub website. He had almost immediately admitted to it and exonerated Polo of having anything to do with it, besides his having made the stupid bet. He had been unaware of his webcam having been activated by Sharod, so they could all watch and see the action, as Sharod has always secretly wanted Celiane. Sharod had gotten off lightly, as far as his criminal situation goes. A year of juvenile probation is what he ended up with. For ruining Celiane's life. But he had been expelled from Lake Worth High and had been forced to go to Surviver Charter School, an alternative school for mostly unreachable or lost cause type of kids.

Sometimes though, Celiane would think about and wonder what their lives could've been like if not for that stupid bet. Would they have stayed married as long as her parents have? Even longer? Been in real love? Soulmates? Have a bunch of kids? Mainly, she wondered if she could have been happy for a long time with Polo. He was handsome and played ball, but in retrospect now, seeing what she saw so clearly now as the Monday morning quarterback, she wondered. He was nowhere near as smart as she. Not even close. He also had absolutely no plan whatsoever, or even an idea about what he might like to do with his life. He didn't care and didn't attempt to even try. Celiane couldn't, in the least bit, begin to comprehend that kind of attitude. To have no idea? None whatsoever? Impossible. She couldn't be like that.

Celiane wanted to be a Marine biologist and had even been interviewed at the Marine Biology Institute in Fort Lauderdale, where she had been told that she was a shoo-in for a good position and scholarship there, possibly even an internship later on. She had always known what her interests are, and she will damn sure be committed to pursuing them. But to Polo, it was all about

63

today, and he never even took the time to think about tomorrow. She could never live like that and wondered how he even could. If he didn't even care about his own future enough to even contemplate it, how could he ever have known that he had wanted a future with her? Simply impossible.

As she did every time, out on one of her walks that she ended up contemplating him, she ended it with the thought that things had actually worked out for the best. Maybe they didn't belong together after all. She just wished she hadn't needed to go through all that pain, the suicide attempt, disappointing her family, and her broken heart. All of that, and for what? To learn that she couldn't trust her man, or any man, for that matter? Well, that wasn't really true, as her mother had found her father when they had both been just kids, living in the streets of Port Au Prince, stealing cookies and bread for survival. She trusted him, and he would never hurt her, they had definitely found theirs, but why couldn't Celiane find her match? Why did Polo have to have been so damn wrong for her? Something inside of her told her to go against her better judgement and go ahead and trust again. It had been a year, and the boys who all chased her now, were inconsistent. Her mom had said that her father had worn her down with persistence. That had eventually won her over, causing her mother to give him a chance.

Maybe that's the trick then, she thought to herself, maybe she just shut every boy down and the right one will just be persistent enough not to ever give up and to keep trying. Plus, it was not like she needed to rush. Just because her mom and dad got together at this age, does not mean that she has to. It just bothered her though. She had enjoyed and gotten used to the attention that Polo had been giving her. The love and adoration. It was nice to have a best friend like that to protect you, love you, cherish you, but then, it always would end up in him hurting you, wouldn't it? Not for my parents, she reminds herself again. So, maybe it was time. Maybe she could give someone a chance. Yea, she smiled to herself decisively, that's what I'm going to do. I'm going to give love another chance. It's not like the situation with Polo would repeat itself. That was just a once-in-a-lifetime experience. She would just have to be a lot more careful. Pay more attention to the signs, keep her walls up to protect herself, and stay guarded. Cautious. Take no chances. Maybe this weekend she could go and check out the Youth Center. None of the boys at Grace Fellowship interested her. Nothing in common. But some of the boys at the Youth Center were nice. She snuck back into the room through her window and fell asleep immediately, her mind having been made up and hoping and dreaming that she would meet a nice boy who wasn't only after sex. One who would like her for the person she really is on the inside.

§§§§

Something unusual happened on that one late Friday night, after an intense yoga and spin class session that Celiane and Nicky had done alone, without Vera there with them, as she was out at the movies with T-Zoe. That same situation was occurring more and more, since Vera left her house with Celiane and Nicky for cover, and would go off with T-Zoe from there. T-Zoe and Vera would meet up with them as soon as the movie was over. Celiane and Nicky crossed the street and entered into the Guatemalan bodega as they always did after a hard workout to get some health shakes to drink on their way to Bryant Park, where they would wait for T-Zoe to drop off Vera, right across from her apartment's location.

"Come on, girl. Damn, that was good money on them stationary bikes! I'm bout to lose all this weight messing with that spin class! I love that shit! I feel like I done sweated a gallon in there, damn," said Nicky, as they walked outside of the bodega after paying for their health drinks.

"Destiny! Hi, Celiane, it's so nice to see you again ... " said a voice, stepping around from the parking lot, and it was the same green-eyed-silver-tongued-devil.

" ... Destiny? That's not my name," said Nicky, her feelings being obviously hurt, thinking that he hadn't remembered her name.

"And I apologize for that. I was actually speaking to Celiane in reference to something we had discussed in a previous conversation we had at the beach last week." He smiled. It was a genuine attempt to open the door.

"The beach?" asked Nicky sotto voce, looking at Celiane.

"You didn't tell me that you had seen him again at the beach. What happened at the beach between you two?"

"Nothing." Celiane rolled her eyes, then looked to Sweets. "What? Are you now following me? How you know I would be here tonight?" she added, giving him an angry and self-righteous look in response.

"Following? No," he said with a hurtful look in response. "I come here every Friday. My mother loves the Pegasus restaurant and so I made it a habit of taking her here on Friday nights."

"Awww! That's so sweet!" said Nicky, elbowing Celiane, who was now looking so sheepish from her previous 'following me' accusation. "Isn't that sweet, Celiane?" Nicky added, smiling her big and healthy smile, insinuating that he was a nice guy for Celiane's benefit, almost promoting Sweets herself.

"I'm sorry, I didn't know. Of course that's sweet, um wow, you know, I really didn't mean that I thought you were following me, it's just that-"

"You thought that I was a stalker!" Sweets joked, laughing and trying to lighten the mood and ease the tension. "It's okay, ma, I guess you just ain't wanna help me with my flat tire after all, huh?"

"Your flat ... ? Oh, yea. Ha-ha-ha," laughed Celiane, trying to get past the awkwardness of the conversation, still embarrassed for accusing him of following her.

"It's okay, ma. As pretty as you are, I'm sure that you have quite a few stalkers, ha-ha-ha," he laughed, trying to put her at ease. "But I only go where I'm welcomed, and if you welcome me, I would love to take you out sometime? Maybe to dinner and a movie? Sound good? Or will your boyfriend get too jeally if I'm your friend too?" He laughed again. He has an easy laugh. A sweet laugh.

"I don't know, I don't really be dating, I-" started Celiane, before Nicky interrupted her, further embarrassing them both.

"Of course! She would love to go out with you, give her your number-"

"Nicky! Oh my God! Can I speak for myself?" said Celiane, clearly irritated. "Okay, I'll give you my number ... "

Chapter Six

Sweets had been plotting and planning all week since seeing Celiane at the beach. After being rejected at the beach, is a more accurate statement in all actuality. She hadn't given him the number that day and left him confused. Confused and put out, actually. But then he just so happened to bring his 'old girl', or mother, to dinner every Friday night to a Greek restaurant that she loved so much that is called Pegasus, so he had that excuse locked in. Just as he expected, he caught her again coming out of the yoga studio, after her class or workout. Her own little thirsty ass friend Nicky, was a better wing man than he could ever ask for. He keeps in mind how her eyes kept cutting down towards his southern region, below his belt level. He decided that he would set a thirst trap for her later on.

"Okay, I got that saved under 'Pretty C', you sure that this your real number, ma?" he asked, smiling with a hint of humor in his smile.

"Yea, I don't have a problem saying 'no', I gave you my number ... " she retorted, leaving the rest of her thought unsaid.

Right then, a light-skinned, raven haired, beautiful woman in her late 30's or early 40's approached them, her own green eyes standing out against the contrast of her dark hair. "Sandino, want to introduce me to your little friends? Simon has some to-go plates for us, are your little friends hungry?" she asked with a genuine smile on her pretty and exotic looking face.

"Um, okay, ladies, this is my mother, Miss Leticia. Mama, this is Pretty-I mean, this is Celiane and her friend, Nicky. She's got a point though, are you guys hungry?" asked Sweets, directing his question to Celiane, well, sweetly.

"No-um, sorry," answered Celiane too quickly, afraid of Nicky possibly accepting his offer of food. "We got our shakes, but thank you for your hospitality, your offer." She offered her most sincere smile.

"Okay, well at least allow me to give you ladies a ride home, okay?" asked Sweets.

"Yes, yes, allow my Sandino to get you safely home. Sandino, I like this one," said Miss Leticia, nodding, indicating toward Celiane. "She is very sweet and has good manners too." She smiled.

Sweets was thinking his plan was seriously working. He knew using his old girl to pull hoes was cheating, borderline 'simping', or using sympathy as a weapon, but it was something that he had to do, as closed off as Celiane is. The difference in her response and attitude, compared to his two previous meetings and now, were astounding. He could feel the actual progress taking place in front of his eyes. If he could get them into Bella, he knew at least Nicky would be impressed, and she would influence Celiane. There wasn't a person on this earth who doesn't love Bella right at first sight.

"Okay, well I guess we can miss our walk back to Bryant Park, Miss Leticia, thank you. We appreciate it a lot ... " Celiane trailed off, beginning to walk with them deeper into the parking lot as another man, Simon, she presumed, brought over two doggie bags to Sweets. They contained styrofoam plates of food. The ones they had apparently offered to Celiane and Nicky to eat. It smelled amazing to her.

As they approached Bella, Sweets hit a button on his key fob and Bella's big engine cranked up with all the TVs, that were currently muted, displaying a music video of Drake and Lil Baby's hit, "Girls Want Girls". It caught Celiane off guard because she had thought, when she had first met Sweets, that he had just been a kid checking out someone else's old school with a few other guys, but now, she has come to find out that this might really be his actual car. That complicates things for Celiane. This was a dope boy's ride. Beautiful, yet dangerous. He is definitely trouble.

She had never before met or hung out with a real dope boy. Her parents had always kept her well hidden. Sheltered. Far away from anything negative or even questionable. So, she felt intrigued. She also had a little hidden resentment for the sheltered life that she had been forced to live. She felt like she wasn't some delicate little flower that could die if left in the sun to burn. She could handle the real world. She is a woman now, not a little girl anymore. She can make her own decisions, and she knows herself, knows she'll make the right choices.

71

"Thank you," said Celiane as Sweets opened the door for her, allowing Nicky to get in the backseat first. A gentleman, thought Celiane. Even if he is a gentleman 'dope boy' at that.

When Celiane sat on the amazing beautiful soft white leather, she felt right at home in the passenger seat. At home-like she belonged. She couldn't believe that Bella had a "21 touch screen Dell computer with WIFI internet right in the dash, with a playstation PS5 connected to it. It was all so amazing to Celiane. It is a car, but the big rims and lift kit obviously made her sit up high like a truck. Bella was truly a piece of art in motion. Beautiful. Celiane could just imagine what the other kids would think if she, Celiane, a poor and humble Haitian girl from the hood, pulled up in a beautiful car like Bella. She allowed herself to imagine pulling up on some of those nasty boys who had participated in posting that embarrassing sex tape online, and flossing in Bella. She would call them up to her in Bella, let them get close enough to touch Bella's door handle, then she would hit the gas and skirt off on them leaving enough rubber, smoke, and exhaust from the loud ass pipes for them to choke on. She smiled to herself.

"You good?" asked Sweets, smiling sweetly, backing out of the parking space.

Celiane smiled up at him, adoration already sparkling in her young and naive eyes, and nodded in the affirmative. He slammed his foot down on the gas after he had turned Drake and Lil Baby's jam up enough to shake the concrete, rocking his four "15

Memphis Audio MOJO speakers. Bella's amazing bored out 427 Corvette engine immediately made the all white, Giovanna rims burn the thin rubber wrapped around them out of the parking lot. Celiane felt like a superstar or celebrity off of her favorite show, *Love and Hip-Hop Miami*. She was in an amazing ride, sitting next to a really nice and good looking guy, and most importantly, she had decided inside of her heart and in her soul, to give love another chance. Maybe to even give Sweets a chance. She couldn't lie to her own self-conscious, which was telling her he was nothing but trouble. His car and swag suggested that he was in the drug game, but there is no way after feeling him, talking to him, vibing with him, that she could possibly not give him a chance. She readily admitted that she was attracted. Not just physically, either.

Celiane was watching him as he drove, his profile, his swag, his confidence. She is attracted to the whole package, his being. The soul that shined through-his aura-and she couldn't understand how she was so on track one day, boys hadn't mattered before him, yet now, it was as if she had been here with him all along. She couldn't understand him, didn't get it one bit, but she knew that there was something here. Maybe even something to this whole 'Destiny' thing that he was always spouting off about. This was the third time that fate, or whatever it was, had brought them together. Three times-so far, that is. Only time will tell what fate holds for them.

"So, what is it that you do, to have such a pretty old school?"

73

asked Nicky, asking really what they both wanted to know, only that she was rude and thirsty enough to ask.

" ... Ha-ha-ha," he chuckled. "A lil' bit of this, and a lil' bit of that ... " he answered her cryptically.

"Um, I'm sorry, but if you are interested in my friend-girl, you gon' have to do a little bit better than that. We don't be doing secrets and shit. Now, keep it real."

" ... Keep it real, huh?" he asked, chuckling again. "First off, I don't know you, and if Pretty C wanna ask me something, I'm sure she will. You, on the other hand, can just sit back and chill. Enjoy Bella's leather and the ride, okay?" As he finished saying his piece, she dropped her jaw damn near down to her lap.

Celiane smiled as she reached back, and with the very tips of her fingers, she pushed Nicky's jaw up, closing her mouth. Nicky was a big girl and wasn't used to being talked to in such a manner. Celiane liked it, she had never seen Nicky shut up without a comeback, and she liked him even more for choosing her, as big girls like Nicky received a lot of attention these days while full figured women are very popular now. It made Celiane feel that much more special, desired, and it gave her a little more in the confidence department, which, despite her pretty face, she was really lacking in. But she felt like she wouldn't be lacking in it for long if she kept hanging out with Sweets. He was a magnet to her and it is something that she isn't able to control, but at this point, she doesn't even want to. He is a light bulb and she-the moth, attracted to his luminescence, his being.

"Okay, so now I'm asking," said Celiane, still smiling from her thoughts. "What is it that you do for a living? And please don't say you own your own business and yada, yada, yada. Cause all dope boys say they own ... they own ... blah, blah, blah, so miss me with that, okay?"

"Okay, okay, you got me. But I'm out of that shit now. All I do now is book appointments, schedule events, and broker deals. Promote. I promote women. I am a womanager. Nothing illegal," he answered, confusing her even more.

"A womanag-huh? What the? What are you talking about?" asked Celiane, now fully intrigued and curious. She wants to know more.

"I'm a womanager, a woman's manager. I book photo shoots, schedule events, ya know? Promote? I'm a manager. You know there are several modeling agencies and film sets in and around Palm Beach, and I'm one of the guys who gets the gigs. I make the deals between the clients and the models, ya know? I'm like an agent, but I manage the payrolls too, ya know?"

"That's so cool," said Nicky, already thirsty for some attention. "Do you think I can be a model? My mom said I modeled for Gerber Baby Food when I was just a baby!"

"Well, sure. They don't discriminate, they hire all shapes and size models for all different types of advertisements or commercials for products or services," answered Sweets diplomatically, while simultaneously shooting shots at her, knowing this girl had a delicate ego that he would need to break sooner or later. "But I was really planning on asking Pretty C to think about modeling. You know, you have quite an incredibly beautiful face, and I know a lot of photographers who could translate your amazing beauty into something profound, something transcendent, ya know?"

Both Celiane and Nicky had their respective mouth hanging wide open in awe, both caught completely off guard, as Sweets pulled up to Bryant Park and found a parking space facing the beautiful inter-coastal waterway. Sweets was completely into his character, completely immersed in his acting job. He loved this part of his job. The actual chase, the game, the macking he does. This is him putting in his work, this is what he truly lives for, his reason for getting up every morning, his specialty. Some people are actors, some singers, some have some imaginations out of this world, enough to create stories, books, screenplays, characters. But not Sweets. No, Sweets is a pimp. And Sweets would always be a pimp. He will fulfill his purpose on this very earth. It's what he is, would always be, and what he loved to be. It's his Destiny.

Chapter Seven

For the next few days after that night with Sweets, Celiane and Nicky didn't talk to each other. Apparently, putting Nicky on the back burner and bringing Celiane up in front on Sweets' agenda had a more adverse than expected reaction. There was a wedge driven between the two, and that had been by his grand design. Sweets was using a version of psychological warfare, and Celiane and Nicky didn't even know they were in a battle yet. Celiane's self-esteem had risen slightly as Nicky's had flatlined, making her even thirstier than normal. She immediately had taken to Facebook, trying to find Sweets with every intention of trying to snag him for herself.

Celiane, on the other hand, had been on Facetime, and had been Snapchatting with Sweets all the while. They had been having deep conversations late into the night, getting to know one another and conversing about anything and everything. Sweets liked to talk to her about his modeling gigs, and seemed to think that she would make an excellent subject, had potential, and could possibly be really successful at it. With his help, of course. Everything is always dependent upon his expertise, his connections.

LAST NIGHT'S FACETIME

"I got a gig for you on Zivity tomorrow. It's a good shoot at a mansion pool, and could possibly give you some income over time, ya know?" said Sweets, as nonchalantly as he possibly could.

"What do you mean? What's its pay? What would I wear?" asked an excited and nervous Celiane.

"Well," started Sweets, trying to sell her on the idea. "Zivity is a Dotcom, and for every time a 'Like' is clicked for any of your pictures, you get five cents and the photographer gets five cents. You get a million clicks, that's $25,000 for you and me to split, me as your womanager, so it's a really good opportunity, and a good pay off over time. Of course it pays bi-monthly, so it's not like you get 25 racks right after the shoot off top, but over time, slowly but surely, as clicks roll in, so does some bread, ya know? More shoots I get you, more chances for more clicks, meaning more money in the end, ya know? It all goes hand in hand."

"It sounds too good to be true. I'm no Naomi Campbell, ya know? Why would anyone want to click on pictures of me? I don't get it ... " Celiane said, trailing off doubtfully. Always second-guessing herself and her ability.

"Are you kidding me? Listen to me, Sweet C. Since I've gotten to know you, I really dig your personality, your intellect, your soul, all of the above, but remember that it was your amazing and beautiful looks and pretty face that attracted me. That's what caught my attention. Now, you are truly beautiful down to your core and in your soul, but pictures can only translate that outer beauty that you have. Remember that. All that inner beauty is all mine, okay baby girl? I'll only be willing to share your looks with the rest of the world." Sweets smiled deeply and added, "The person inside is my girl."

"You want me to be your girl?" she asked shyly. She was honestly surprised. She had started thinking that he was only interested in trying to recruit her for his own agency, or whatever it was, and just wanted her to model to make money. Now he was making it clear that he was interested in her inner being, her personality, her inside qualities, all that is important to her. It is exactly what she had always wanted to hear, what she had always wanted to be noticed for. She wanted to be someone's number one. Someone's first choice.

"Of course I do, did you think I was just fishing for models to manage?" Sweets finally answered sarcastically, making her heart flutter. "Why?" he asked suddenly, as if being self-consciously humble and almost giving off an innocent and shy vibe that very few actors could successfully pull off, immediately disarming her. "Don't you want to be my girl? I just thought that ... since we got along so well, ya know?"

"Of course I want to be your girl! It's all I've ever wanted since we met!"

"Oh, good," he said. "Don't scare me like that, Sweet C. You gon' give me a heart attack and break my heart. You know I'm feelin' you like I've never felt with anyone else before in my life. It's like I've known you all of my life, Sweet C." She laughed happily at this statement. "Why you laughin'?"

"Because I feel the exact same way about you," she replied, her soul smiling.

§§§§

Sweets picked up Celiane for her first Zivity shoot and was driving her there while gently conversing with her about the shoot, among other things. He was really trying to give her some more motivation in order to get her into his stable. She wasn't going to just jump into the lifestyle, so she had to be given steps. Like a child learning to walk, she would have to be able to take one step at a time, and as her teacher, he would need to guide her, one step at a time. She would need motivation though, so he needed a competitor, first step.

"So, Nicky hit me on Facebook and she is asking me to hook her up on a gig for modeling, and ... I didn't wanna do it without talking to you first, so you know what's going on and you can decide how you wanna play it. I just didn't wanna keep anything from you," said Sweets, gently planting the seeds of competition in her head, while keeping her on point with her own friend.

"So, can you? I mean get her a gig? Will you?" she asked him as he drove.

"Of course, Sweet C, she's your friend! Of course I'll help her out, I would do anything for you and more. Anything at all ... " he said, feeding into it even more.

80

"Oh, well okay. When is she going to be doing her shoot?" she asked, confused and unsure about how she felt about Nicky modeling, or much about how she felt about her being around her new boyfriend. She saw Nicky's reaction, to not only him, but also her reaction to Celiane. She already knew that Nicky was thirsty, but she was her friend, she wouldn't have to worry about her being around her new boyfriend. Or would she?

"Oh, don't worry about it, I'll have her in a different type of shoot. She's going to be doing plus size or BBW shoots, it's a different photographer. Okay, we're here," said Sweets, as they pulled up to a really nice house on Manalapan, a town east of Lantana, located on the inter-coastal side, as opposed to the beach side.

"Why is there a realtor sign in front? Whose house is this?" asked Celaine.

"Don't worry about it, most photographers and film makers have deals worked out where they break off the realtor, and we use the mansion, or the condo balcony, to do photoshoots and film scenes. Nobody lives in this house ... " Sweets said.

"Oh, okay. Well, it's a beautiful house ... I'm a little nervous," said Celiane, as they sat in the car, in front of the house. She laughed nervously, not knowing what to do with their hands.

"It's okay, Sweet C, I'll be there the entire time, till you get the hang of it, and I'll help direct you, you got nothing to worry about, baby. You are beautiful. So pretty, bae, it's so easy. Just try to relax," he said, reaching in the glove box and taking a pill from a small brown bottle that he pulled out. "Here, take this pill, baby. It will relax you."

"What is this?" she asked, as he put the long french fry-shaped pill in her hand.

"It's just a bar, baby. Take it. It will help with your anxiety. All models and actresses take them to feel more comfortable and suppress the nervousness. Here, wash it down with this-I ain't got no water here," he said, handing her a prescription bottle of a liquid. "It's just some cough syrup, it will help to get the pill down and clear your mind."

"Are you sure? Okay, I definitely need this. I am super nervous," she said.

Celiane popped the bar, and chased it with some promethazine with codeine lean. Sweets smiled at her and pop kissed her on her lips tenderly, as he took her hand into his own, leading her out of Bella and up to the front door of the mini-mansion. After ringing the bell, a tall, slim, white guy opened the door.

"Hi, I'm Jordan Jewels, come on in ... " he said, moving aside to let them in. Celiane almost gasped at the interior decorations inside. It is simply stunning.

Inside the house, there was filming and camera equipment and accessories everywhere. There were a few other girls there, all of them white, with blonde hair and blue eyes. All but one of them wearing flowing robes, and that one had some extremely risqué negligee on. Celiane hoped that they weren't expecting her to wear such revealing attire. She was pretty sure that she would never feel that comfortable with her body. Didn't see how any girl could be that confident with herself, but as she took in all of these girls, so she can see why immediately. They were beautiful with their hair and stick figure bodies. Celiane is slim-thick, but she has some amazing curves at least, but then, that's what models really looked like. Sticks with big hair. Not her though, she felt like she didn't belong. This wasn't her, she was not that pretty, not like these girls were.

"Oh my God, look at them," said Celiane. "I can't do this, I'm not as-" He interrupted her right there.

"Sweet C, you are even more beautiful than they are, way badder! Trust me, bae, I do this for a living and I would never steer you wrong. Remember? This is my job," he said and then led her over to a robed Barbie doll that looked like Rachel McAdams on the movie *Mean Girls*. He pulled the tie on her robe and opened it. "Tiffany, show her what you got, girl," he said, smiling confidently.

The Barbie dropped her robe with her erect nipples on her C-cups, plainly uncovered, her rib cage poking out prominently, and she started to pose with only some Victoria's Secret panties on her small-skinny frame. She smiled easily with perfect teeth, bent over, turned around, knelt down, tweaked her nipples with her thumb and index fingers and then laid back on the couch sexily and spread her legs. "It's so easy girl, this is your first time, right? Girl, take a bar, just relax, and sit back and let it flow, you are gorgeous! You'll have no problem," said Tiffany, the Barbie, who has been modeling since she was Celiane's age as a teen model by the name, Teen Tiffany.

"I already gave her a bar, so she should be good in a few minutes. Hey, Tiffany, can you hook her up in wardrobe while I talk to Jordan about her set?" asked Sweets.

"Sure, Sweets." She smiled really big for him. Flirting, Celiane realized. "C'mon, girl. I'll show you around ... " said Tiffany.

It was obvious to Celiane that Sweets was well-known and liked here, so she felt a little bit more comfortable than she thought she would normally. She followed Tiffany to the bedroom, which upon entering it, she saw that it was packed with boxes of panties, bras, and even fish nets and stockings were located all around the room in every space that they could fit them in. The bed was covered in heels and thigh-high boots, both plastic and leather, and even some snow boots and roller skates, surprisingly. Apparently, they did every shoot known to man here. It was incredible. Celiane was dizzy.

"You can shower in that bathroom, bathing suits are in this box here," Tiffany said, indicating a box by the closet. "We change in here and all that. I think he scheduled you for a bathing suit set, so pool and outside shower. Damn, you must be really new. Anyways, if you want rings bracelets, watches, and necklaces, they are all in those boxes over there. Don't try to waste time keeping them, they are all fake." She was pointing to each jewelry box as she spoke.

"Um, so what do I wear? What do I do in the scene?" asked Celiane.

"Oh! You are so sweet! And cute too! I didn't think you were that new. Just pick a two piece bathing suit, preferably a microkini for maximum clicks, and your manager and Jordan will do the rest. Good luck!" said Tiffany, and then, off she went, bouncing all bubbly out of the bedroom door, leaving Celiane by herself again.

Celiane went through all she could in this big box full of skimpy beach wear and just couldn't find one that wasn't some dental floss with a cotton swab sewed onto it. She couldn't believe real life girls could wear some of these things. She finally settled on a white bikini that barely covered her nipples. The white brought out her beautiful ebony skin, making her look like a princess or queen. She had done her own make up at Vera's house, where she was spending the night tonight, and she was laughing out loud at the 'bat wing' fake eye lashes that Vera had given her to wear to make her even more exotic than she felt she really was. They were so damn ridiculous that she started giggling while just looking at them in the vanity mirror. The pill must have taken effect, she thought to herself, because now, suddenly she was feeling so relaxed, so calm, like nothing mattered. For some strange reason, she just knew and felt like everything would work out just fine. She smiled at herself. She felt really pretty, very sexy. Without even knowing it, she actually felt the very definition of sexy.

She walked outside of the wardrobe room, and in through the living room. She stepped outside feeling loose, feeling loved, as she looked from Sweets to Jordan. They both smiled at her, loving the way she looked obviously. She smiled back and walked over to them, and shook the offered hand by Jordan Jewels, her new photographer. He has kind eyes, she thought to herself. Tall, blonde, and very handsome. Light skin, but wearing it well with muscles in a tank top and cargo shorts, standing at about 6 foot tall, she immediately felt comfortable with him.

"Nice to meet you, Celiane. I'm Jordan again. Now, what we are going to do-since this is your first time, is do some pool and sunbathing shots, maybe something more fun if you'd like, but, are we doing all of them as non-nudes, or ... ?" asked Jordan, looking at Sweets for an answer to his confusing inquiry.

"Ah, well," said Sweets, looking at Celiane. "We can start with non-nudes and see where that takes us, huh? Okay, yea, let's see where we go from there ... "

Celiane listened only halfway to their conversation, not really even understanding the industry terms or the direction that the conversation was taking. Not really caring, as all of a sudden, she was so comfortable, so positively sure of herself, she was going to actually enjoy this shoot. She can feel it, this might be what she was meant to do. Her xanax bar and lean having taken full effect on her, she was becoming fully relaxed, absolutely calm, like an early Sunday morning on Lake Worth Beach, ocean flat, without waves or wind blowing. As the men talked, she walked over to the folding pool chair and thought back to Tiffany, with the poses and motions that she had so easily performed and displayed, showing her sexuality, her sensual inner being, her gracefulness. Talent that she had been born with but never realized that she actually possessed. Something she wouldn't overlook anymore.

Celiane heard her favorite Jacquees song, "Who's", playing in her head, or was a radio playing? As she moved her body almost snake-like. She wasn't even moving consciously. In her mind's eye she was relaxed at the beach, playing in the water. Subconsciously, she knew that somewhere outside of her brain, that the conversation had been suddenly and effectively terminated, and instead, had been substituted with a constant clicking.

CLICK! CLICK! CLICK! CLICK!

It was now the beat in her head playing. The more clicks and the faster they came, the more moves and more dancing she was doing. She was moving so slowly, yet at such a natural pace that the camera didn't even have to do too much to be able to stay up and capture all of the many original and exotic poses, and all of her sensual body in them.

Celiane went from softly dancing into posing, just as Tiffany had showed her. She was looking directly into the camera, and started to make love to it. She went from biting her bottom lip to licking her lips. It was as if she had always been in front of a camera, or born to be in front of one, and knew exactly how to turn and the perfect facial expressions to make to match her body's moves. She put her feet in the air and spread her legs, opening her gates, inviting the photographer, and in turn, her fans, into her loving and sensual body. The world of her sexuality.

"Okay, good! Good! Now, get into the water and get wet ... shit, lose the top too, take it off slowly and look at the camera, don't smile. Bite the lip," said Jordan.

Celiane reached for her string tied bikini top, but before she did, she looked over to Sweets, suddenly unsure of herself.

"It's okay, baby. Go ahead. Keep going, you're doing great, " said Sweets.

Chapter Eight

Sweets knew he had to get Celiane to take the molly. There is no ands, ifs or buts about it. But he still has to take baby steps with his new 'prime', his pet project. She wouldn't do any of the things that he wanted her to do until he got her to loosen up a little bit. In other words, until he got inside of her head. Controlled her thoughts. She had to loosen up, trust, and get comfortable with him, in front of a camera, and in front of random people. She had taken the first step really well. She had been completely and totally agreeable to everything so far, to his suggestions, and that was very important to Sweets. She had taken the xanax bar and sipped the lean without second-guessing or asking too many questions. That in itself is a big move. He could've been like any other guy, crushed the xanax and put it in a shot of Hennessy, or better still, Jager, since almost all girls loved Jager Bombs. But no, Sweets couldn't do that. He can't try to force it with his prime, he has to finesse her. That's what a real pimp does. Finesse. A womanager is a finesser of everyone around him. He hates the word 'manipulator'. He finesses not only his girls, but also clients, other industry participants such as film makers, photographers, even lawyers, doctors, realtors, basically anyone that he comes into contact with.

Sweets couldn't put anything in her drink, that would be against his principles and morals. He would instead finesse her into taking molly next time when she complains about the bar and lean. If she doesn't remember anything, like a lot of people who mix bars with other drugs or alcohol, she might not want to try it again. The confusion-type of a hangover was always a regretful experience, but that would be his reason to introduce her to the new designer drug, molly. He needed her to take the bar and lean this first time, for her to get mentally loose and ready to get this first shoot out of the way and some content online to start bringing in some income. It wouldn't be much, but then again, Sweet C's young, sweet, and innocent look that she has about her, might turn her into an instant hit. Kind of how Andiland's Andi Pink did in her first photoshoot in Winnipeg. Only time would tell, but this is just a part of the process. Once she actually saw her first pictures online, and he started spending money on her, she would definitely start to loosen up and see the benefit in being on his team, in his stable. But it would take a series of steps, and right now he was still on the beginning steps. Baby steps, and she, still an infant in the business, trying to learn her first steps.

It would work in the same way with the sex. Most people thought that it was the other way around, but in reality, it was the girl who had to make the first moves on Sweets. He would not just give up the dick. She must impress him, work towards earning it. So, while Celiane would be there with her defenses on high alert and dreading his making a move on her like most boys did, he never would. She would always mentally be preparing an excuse for why she didn't want to have sex, and yet, the feared moves would never come. After a while, when the girl gets so comfortable around him, she would relax, after seeing that he wasn't going to make a move on her, and she would in turn start to catch some sort of feelings and emotions toward him, she would then be ready and want him to make a move, when she was finally in need of his physicality, his love, his touch. But still, he wouldn't make that expected move, pretending love and respect for her. A willingness to wait for her, to earn her trust.

On and on it would go, until she would get exasperated and start hinting physically. Maybe rubbing her ass on his pelvis while they spoon, laying on a couch watching a movie, kissing him more deeply than ever before. Trying to be more sexy, more appealing, yet not understanding that the physical attraction wasn't the problem. Then would come the insecurities. The self-questioning. Why doesn't he make a move? Am I pretty enough? Am I sexy? Doesn't he like me? Am I not attractive or something? What is it? What's wrong with me? Why doesn't he want me?

In all actuality, what it really would be is, that when she did well at a shoot, session, or shift, whichever he had her working at, he would act impressed, happy, grateful and want to reward her. Using Celiane's analogy in dog terms, when a dog would learn a new trick or please her master, she could be rewarded for such a job well done and for accomplishing something great and pleasing him.

It is in this same way that Sweets would reward his girls with dick. It was her treat for making a large amount of money or for doing something impressive. It is something that a womanager doesn't give out easily. Talk about 'hard to get', Sweets plays his game of 'damn near impossible to get', and only he knows why. Control. Pussy is a woman's natural power source. Whole superpowers in world history have fallen behind some extraordinary pussy. If the need for a woman's pussy was taken out of the equation, so is a woman's power. Sweets doesn't need pussy. He knows that his dick and his mouth have been the power because he has taken the availability of his dick away from them. It is used for a tool or reward only, depending on what the situation calls for. A tool if it is a time when he has to do due diligence and convince one of his girls that she is loved and is a cherished part of his team, his stable, and that it couldn't run smoothly without her and her contribution to him and his world, his cause, his dream. He has used his dick as a tool many times over, while trying to convince one of his girls to chase his dream with him. To give her his all, because one day, she would be a part of their empire, the world that they had built together. But until then, his dick must be a reward for something, or a tool for something else. He could not give it away freely, and would never even dream about giving it away outside of his stable for free. This would become a later problem with Nicky. Something he would need to deal with, and soon.

After Celiane's first shoot, she felt so good, so sexy and beautiful, that she couldn't wait at all for her next shoot, so Jordan offered to do a couple more sets then and there. He couldn't believe how Celiane made love to the camera just as Emily Browning had done to captivate her audience in the fan favorite movie, *Sucker Punch*. He never before saw such captivating and inviting movements and poses on a virgin shoot. Or on any shoot, for that matter. He wanted to make a few more sets, so they did a boat scene on the '27 open fisherman docked on the back canal that led to the inter-coastal waterway. She did magnificent there, as well as at the shower scene set that they did afterwards. The single drops of water being frozen in time by the high shutter speed of the professional Cannon camera. Both sets came out amazingly successful.

§§§§

While Jordan and Celiane were doing the pool scene and then the sunbathing scene sets previously, Sweets had noticed how comfortable Sweet C had become in front of the camera, and decided to go ahead and see to Nicky's shoot, leaving Celiane grudgingly in Jordan Jewels' care. Her shoot was at the nude beach in the City of Miami Beach, called Halover Beach. He decided not to be delicate with Nicky-since she had already hit his Facebook page and DM on Instagram numerous times, practically begging. She knew today is Sweet C's photoshoot day too, since she is at Vera's house right now, where he had picked Celiane up from earlier, and since Vera and T-Zoe were waiting with Nicky, Sweets figured she already knew. This is good, he thought to himself.

"Hey, sexy," said Nicky, being extra thirsty and flirtatious, now that Celiane wasn't around. She is really so thirsty that she would do anything for his attention and she made it obvious.

"C'mon, get in," he said impatiently. "You know I'm only

doing this cause your Sweet C's friend, right?"

She was startled by his bluntness, but quickly got into Bella and he floored it.

"Wha? Huh? Why you say that? Don't you think I look good?" she asked.

"You a'ight, but I have to drive you all the way to Miami to the damn nude beach. I couldn't find anything for you locally in Palm Beach, so I hope you ain't just wasting my time. Celiane act like she ain't wanna show nothing, so I hope you ain't all bourgeois too, trying to hide under all them clothes and shit. It's a nude beach, ya know?" he said, acting like he is truly put out while also hitting her self-esteem as well, a part of his elaborate game that he is laying down for her benefit.

"Shit, I'm a freak! I'll show it all off! I ain't scared of nothin'! Boy-bye with all that!" she said, trying to sound all grown at only 17 years old. While at the red light, before getting onto the interstate I-95, he hit Bella's drop top button, unfolding her convertible top, so that the wind wouldn't be too bad when he is speeding on the slab, or I-95.

"Shit, you gone have to show me 'bout that, girl. Y'all be actin' all young and shit, I might gotta see some ID, make sho' your ass grown!" he said, laughing out loud.

"Shit, boy, how's this for grown?" she asked, and as he got onto I-95, she went immediately to begin unbuttoning his pants. Once she started unbuttoning them, he knew that all of his mental and emotional gymnastics had been working on her. Driving a wedge between Nicky and Celiane would make things easier and that much better for him. They would now fight for his attention, both wanting to please him more than the other.

"Oh, wow. .. mmm," said Nicky, as she pulled out her desired toy from within the confines of his pants and began licking the head of his dick. "It's so big and beautiful."

She put his head into her waiting warm and salivating mouth. He instantly began to grow to attention. She swirled her tongue ring around his head and shaft, making him become rock hard, standing his full 9 inches like a statue. As he got into the fast lane and floored the petal, he thought about what she said about being a freak. She worked her tongue ring like a pro, flicking it on his head, then shoving his whole rod up to his implanted pearl, down deep into her throat. She wasn't lying at all there. He said to himself, 'might as well test the waters ...

He put his hand on the back of her head and began to shove his entire length down the back of her throat, with his other hand on his Grant woodgrain steering wheel. She took it all, and then even started cupping his balls in her hand, taking even more of him into her deep throat. He kept the car speeding at about 90 miles per hour, going crazy to hold back his nut, and was essentially gag-fucking her, making her eyes tear up and almost fatally choking her on his dick. Chancing a quick look to visualize the feeling he was getting, he saw immediately that her other hand was in her pants, fingering herself, bringing herself to her own climax while he was still gag-fucking her. That did it for him and he could no longer hold it back. He finally let go of his nut, coming all the way down her throat and into her belly right then in that moment.

§§§§

As soon as Sweets got to Halover Beach, the nude beach in Miami, there were several other models there walking around naked, and so he quickly stripped down and then told Nicky to follow suit.

"It's a nude beach, Nicky, you gotta get naked," he has said to her and was just trying to get a reaction out of her, as there is no rule about having to be naked on Halover Beach, it was simply that nudity isn't illegal there. She had thrown him for a loop earlier when she had sucked his dick as if she was trying to win a competition or maybe attempting to suck a golf ball through a garden hose. Either way, he now had no doubt whatsoever that Nicky is a champ and has no inhibitions at all to speak of.

He didn't need to give her a bar, but he did anyway, simply because he wanted her loose and doing her best work, as he was actually doing Jermaine a favor, the photographer, and had asked for one in return, for Jermaine to do a couple shoots for him, for his OnlyFans pages for his girls, so he wanted all of his money's worth. Videos he would sometimes do on his own, sometimes even using the surveillance cameras at Relax and just blurring out the customers' faces from the images. Other times he would use professional PornHub film crews, like Bang Bros, who used to have Kimbo Slice as a camera man. He was going to go full speed ahead and straight turn Nicky out. She didn't need steps like Sweet C, she is a cum guzzling slut and ready to put that work in. He was actually contemplating taking her straight to Thug Mansion, which is what they all called his house, where he keeps all of his girls in the Black Diamond neighborhood, out West, in Wellington, and giving her a chance straight away in his little stable. Sweet C, on the other hand, would take a month or so, he thought to himself. He hopes that it will be no longer than that.

Nicky is already buck naked, she talked and was being playful with the other girls already. Apparently, the coolers were filled with Corona Extra beers for the film crews and models and Nicky had already started drinking one. Not good to drink on top of xanax and codeine lean. He needed to get her under control immediately, since she was simply trying to impress him ever since the amazing dick sucking marathon that had taken place on the ride down to Miami and his challenge to compare her to Sweet C. He had come twice in her mouth and couldn't believe what she could do with her tongue ring. Then she rubbed his nut all in her face when he finally had busted the second time and made sure to look up at him with her cum painted face. He was pretty damn impressed, if he did say so himself, so he couldn't resist getting a quick picture of it with his iPhone 14. She definitely has a lot of potential, and he would be sure to make use of all of it, and share it with all of his chubby chaser clients. She is very experienced and equally uninhibited.

Jermaine started taking some tentative pictures of Nicky, as

97

she runs naked into the waves, came back out soaking wet and walked back toward the camera sexily. She then dropped down to her hands and knees, crawling toward the camera like a Florida Panther, crawling silently and stealthily toward its prey. Unexpectedly, she was actually doing pretty good as such an inexperienced model. She turned over, rolling around in the sand as the click-click, click-click of Jermaine's camera captured all of her essence. The purity of her sexuality and outer being that she was continuously sharing with the camera with the future observers, was very profound and beautiful. She, a real show piece.

Again Sweets was impressed. But he wanted to push her to her limits to see how far she would go. To see if he can make her say "don't", "stop", or "can't". Most of the other models were gone by now, and the others were gathering their things and were ready to leave, not paying them any attention at all. He decided to push her all the way. "Spread your lips, rub your nipples, play with yourself! C'mon, Nicky. Enough messing around," said Sweets, immediately drawing a look from Jermaine. There wasn't supposed to be any sexual acts being performed or committed on Halover Beach, but he looked right back at Jermaine, silently communicating his will to him, ordering him to go hard or go home. Nothing less than full speed would be accepted with Sweets.

Jermaine said nothing as he continued to click away. Nicky spread her pussy lips, her eyes closed, and rubbed her pearl. She used her other hand to rub on her D-cups and tweak her nipples. With her other hand, she then inserted two fingers into her fleshy, shaved pussy. She is very pale, curvy and voluptuous. Her ass poking out as she rolled onto her stomach and was finger-banging herself from the back. Jermaine was not missing a beat, knowing the value of these pictures in this set. She wasn't bucking, so Sweets went even farther and handed her the empty Corona bottle. "Use this, Nicky. Go slow," Sweets roughly ordered her.

Nicky turned around again, sitting on her ass and inserted the bottle slowly and sensually, then began the back and forth. In and out of the bottle. Since the bottle was so perfectly clear, Jermaine zoomed in on the long neck of the bottle which allowed the inside of her big pussy lips to be seen through the glass. Her clear cum and pussy juices started to accumulate at the bottom of the bottle, as well as dripping in between her mountainous ass cheeks and puddling into the beach sand. She kept it going for a good ten minutes, bringing herself to a climax several times. Jermaine was actually into it. He was very surprised with her performance, and they both saw the cum and juices that had entered the top of the Corona bottle and had started to collect at the bottom and started to fill the lower part of the Corona with her juices.

Sweets sees that Nicky's being high on xanax and lean did nothing to stop her from noticing the attention she was getting. She loved every minute of their attention. She definitely wanted Sweets for her own man, and she knew that this was the way to his heart. She knows the kind of man he is and what he finds valuable. She can see his expression and him being naked, she knew that she had him turned on, she just needed to lock him in. She needed to give it to him so raw that he would stay on her line. There was no way that Celiane's almost virgin ass could handle all of that dick that Nicky had just sucked and fallen in love with. It could be all of hers, and she knows that she can handle every bit of it. In fact, she wants to handle every inch of it and keep it for herself. She has taken even bigger dicks than his before, and knew how deep her pussy is, knows what she can do with it, she would show him, then make him love her, she thought to herself.

While Jermaine was clicking away, his jaw was still damn near to the ground with the show that she is putting on. He is in for a big surprise, she thought to herself, as she turned over, back to them, facing the beach waves, and got onto her hands and knees again. She had left a puddle in the dry sand that she had just been playing with herself on, and her Corona bottle was still collecting even more of her juices. She let the bottle stick out of her pussy from the back and she began to make her ass clap, which in turn was making the Corona bottle in her pussy bounce up and down like T-Pain's song, UpDown. She is a pro with her kegels, so her pussy locked the bottle in its grip. The bottle was basically fucking her while she made her ass clap. Jermaine stopped clicking, as she was moaning and fucking herself with the bottle, astonished. Sweets punched his arm. "Keep goin', dumbass!" He raised his camera again in answer and the clicking of it resumed, capturing every jaw-dropping moment of this amazing scene.

She came again and again. She is insatiable. Sweets never saw a girl cum so much before, but he knew she is a certified money making slut, so he smiles to himself, acknowledging what he now has in his possession. She stopped long enough to rearrange herself with a split while on top of the bottle, riding it. She has a hand in the sand for balance and her weight is on the bottle now, the other hand playing with her clit, making her juices flow even more. Even though the Corona bottle has its bottom in the sand, she had come so many times and produced so much of her own juices, that it was still able to display the cum level as a quarter of the bottle being full. It is amazing. Sweets is just so flabbergasted-he was hooked from the first click of the camera. There is no way that he is going to allow this girl to end up with any other player than him. She would be his property. He was going to make her his top webcam attraction for his OnlyFans and PornHub accounts.

She came another time, and finally laid back, being all the way out of breath and trying to catch it. She slowly took the bottle out of her pussy and then smiled sexily at the camera, but really for Sweets' benefit. She then wiped the sand off of the bottom of the bottle, showed it to the camera, a little more than a quarter full. "Watch this baby," she said to Sweets, looking him dead in the eyes as Jermaine continued to click-click away. Next, she took the bottle and tipped it up, swallowing up all of the foamy clear juices and cum that her own beautiful pussy had produced for their pleasure-their show.

"Wow! That was amazing," Jermaine told her, clapping, smiling, fully amazed at her ability to come up with something original and interesting at the same time on her first shoot ever.

"Yea, Nicky. Good job," said Sweets, downplaying it, as he walked off to text Jordan to let him know what was up. This had taken longer than expected and he didn't trust that Zivity guy for a second unsupervised with his new prime, Sweet C. It wouldn't surprise him one bit if that damn playa hater would try to throw salt in his game and try to pull a 'GTH' or Grand Theft Hoe, trying to knock Celiane for himself. He doesn't think he should have to worry too much though, as he knows that salt kills snails, not real playas. He also knows and has faith that his game is 'Pimp Tight' like MJG, but one could never be too careful with his prime, so he can never close his eyes to another playas' game. Sweets is absolutely convinced that as his prime, Celiane could take his stable all the way to the next level, but he had to keep a clear head. He couldn't let feelings or emotions get in the way of his game. He had to treat her like a princess, in this honeymoon-type phase, but he had to walk a tight rope, as he couldn't have feelings for her, even though he obviously liked her. What was there in her not to like? He thought to himself. She is smart, funny, cute, sexy, totally cool... Of course, he likes her. If he didn't have to play his position, he would have wanted to date her, but everything has its place, just as he has his and Celiane has hers: in his stable. Business is business, and business always comes first. Money always comes first.

Chapter Nine

Celiane had been modeling for hours, had changed clothes so many times it made her head spin, and she had completed four different sets. According to Jordan, she had done an amazing job at it too. Her photographer, Jordan, is a whole sweetheart and a Godsend for her. He was very particular and vocal in his craft and that alone was enough to get Celiane immediately on his program. She listened to his praise and he made her proud of her hard work. Overall though, she enjoyed the work, was having a good time doing it in fact, and is consistently building her confidence as she went with each successful shoot that she completed. Jordan enjoyed the fact that Celiane wasn't aware of exactly how amazingly beautiful she is. Her lips and smile are similar to that of Megan Good, while her complexion, legs and ass resembled that of the famous tennis player, Serena Williams, who actually lives down the street from this very house, in nearby Palm Beach Gardens.

Jordan was doing an amazing job at bringing Celiane's beauty and sexuality to life in his photos, especially without them becoming something lewd or cheap. She was very sensual, pretty and is just a stunning all around model, and a pleasure to work with as far as Jordan is concerned and he knows that she could make a real living, modeling, if she wanted to. Jordan suggested starting an Instagram account while they sat outside enjoying a delivery pizza on their dinner break, after so many hours of shooting sets.

"I want to try one more set if you want, an inside set, I have the living room or bedroom already set and lighted, if you want to try, what do you say?" he asked her.

"Sure, why not? What should I wear? And what happened to Sweets?" she asked, looking all around for him.

"Oh, he'll be back soon, they're already done with the other shoot, I am sure your friend did really great, his texts said she had a successful shoot, and in industry terms, that's as good as it gets," said Jordan, already trying to throw salt in the game. He really wants Celiane for himself and doesn't understand why she would be with this pimp nigga, Sweets, in the first place. So, throwing salt in the game is his only recourse to combat Sweets' pimp tight game.

"Oh, so he went to Nicky's shoot?" asked Celiane, almost dejectedly, visibly concerned about the necessity of Sweets being around Nicky without her there with them.

"Yea, that nude beach in Miami, but he should be back soon," said Jordan. "But I bet your friend didn't get as much done as we did today! More pictures equals more 'likes' and more money for both of us on Zivity. You know, if you stay working with me, I can take you far in this business and keep you safe, okay? Alright then, let's get one more set done, okay? Then we'll call it a night and maybe have some drinks, whadayasay?"

"Alright, but what should I wear on this inside shoot?" she asked.

"Whatever you want to wear, but just my little suggestion would be that you can do business lady with the shoulder pads in

104

the business suit and come down to the stockings and garter belts, thongs, teddy, whatever you want. But I'll have to set up the office scene, or you can do schoolgirl or cheerleader in the living room, or even co-ed in the bunk beds in the dorm room set up. You pick, but remember, I'll have to set up the lights in the office if you want to do the business lady-business suit," said Jordan.

"What about the kitchen? Is the lighting in there good enough?" she asked as she already had an idea from what she had seen in wardrobe, her instincts telling her to go against the norm and be different.

"Hells yea, it's really good in there ma. The lighting in there is actually brighter."

"Okay, I have an idea, and it's cute, I think you'll like it," she said, quickly before running off.

Celiane went to the wardrobe room and got undressed, completely naked and stared at her body in the full length mirror for a few moments. She has awakened many things in herself today that she had never been in touch with. She finally could see that her body was truly a beautiful thing, and that she maybe is actually special. Maybe she could be a model. She could see it now, and believe it too. Maybe even believe in herself. She finally had started to gain some confidence in herself. She could hear Jordan moving things around the house, preparing for the shoot. She knows that she is truly ready for this. Made for this in fact.

Celiane grabbed the 3x white T-shirt with the words on the

front. She loved this shirt. She slipped it on over her naked body and smiled at herself in the mirror. The shirt came to just a few inches below her shaved vagina. All of her beautiful ebony skin on her thighs and bare legs were showing, her tiny and pretty feet prominent with her pink toenail polish on, her cute little baby toes, making her look girl-next-door cute. She slipped on a new pair of plain white panties that were so light that they were almost sheer. The way her vagina lips folded in made her beautiful slit look as if it was nothing more than a crease in her beautifully perfect ebony skin. Perfection that had always been hidden from her, yet wasn't anymore.

"'Good Girls Are Just Bad Girls Who Haven't Been Caught'? I like it. It takes a little bit away from your sweet and innocent look, but, I like it," said Jordan, as he admired the message her shirt had printed on it. When she gets to the kitchen, he was almost done setting up his camera equipment without the lighting, after running tests with light filters and scanners, showing that the kitchen's florescent lighting in the ceiling was very bright and plenty of light for their purposes. She explored the appliances and sink while he finished up and noticed some whip-cream in the refrigerator. She began messing around in the kitchen sink, when Jordan finally indicated that he was ready to shoot.

She started out shyly and playfully. In only panties and T-shirt, she grabbed a coffee cup and did some morning-after-sex poses. Then she switched gears, putting the sexy I'm-a-dirty-girl look on, and tying up the bottom of the T-shirt , playing on the floor matts, doing splits, and then grabbing her ankles, standing up. She did that famous 'Face-Down-Ass-Up' handstand, then she got up onto the counter and lifted her ass off of it and allowed Jordan to get some up close and personal shots on her panties and then she pulled them between her lips to show an incredibly deep, yet amazingly perfect and pretty camel toe, one of the inmate fans in prison's favorite shots to have in the pen. Something for them to fantasize about her with.

While on top of the counter, she got on her hands and knees and allowed Jordan to capture her sexiness and innocence all at once. She crawled like that over to the sink and grabbed the removable spray nozzle, smiling a naughty smile. She turned it on playfully, Jordan not missing a beat, and started squirting water on her white T-shirt, right where her nipples are, just for them to be able to show through. They immediately hardened, poking out like prominent beads up high on her chest. As he photographed this, she played and tweaked her nipples mischievously with two fingers for the camera, beginning to shed her innocence and bring in a new feeling of liberation.

Click-Click! Tweek. Click! Click! Tweek. Click!

Finally, she squatted over the sink as Jordan took high-speed moving shots, making each drop of water that was hitting her white panties and already swelling lips-that made up the prettiest camel toe ever, seem as if each drop of water were a separate celebration altogether. She rubbed on top of her panties with two fingers in order to produce a response for the camera's benefit. She was surprised at just how wet she was getting, notwithstanding the fact that she was running the warm faucet water over her panties. Something was changing in her, something became alive for her and made her want to break her abstinence pact. In her mind, she was already breaking it while thinking about Sweets and his amazing green eyes, being so wet.

She slid her hand inside of her panties and began to play in her pussy. Jordan didn't miss a beat and was shooting nonstop. He loved a girl who loves her work. This girl isn't just some 'starfish', laying there, waiting for him to do all of the work, she was alive and in action, making love to the camera and setting the scenes. She was now sliding her fingers in and out of her pussy, yet doing so underneath her white cotton panties, which for some reason, made it even hotter for Jordan. For viewers that wanted to see Celiane in this position doing this to herself. Fans.

She started to moan, her body's bucking onto her fingers made it all the more real to Jordan. The bars really had her coming and creaming all inside of her simple white cotton panties. He kept snapping, capturing all of the clear thick cum, spilling out around the seat of her panties that was in between her perfectly beautiful ass cheeks. She continued going and sat inside the sink and closed her eyes, while rubbing her nipples with her forearm and making herself even more sexy, more wet, if that was even physically possible.

Sweets, for some fateful reason, chose that very moment to walk in, and he was immediately turned on. All promises of making

Celiane wait for, and earn the dick, now out of the window. He watched while she took off the shirt and starts posing again using her hair, fingers, forearm, and finally, some of the whip-cream she had found in the refrigerator, to conceal her nipples and keep her pictures as non-nudes, which will have a lot more views and even more hits. Nudes are required by law to be kept to only 18 and over viewers, so non-nudes do much better, and they are allowed to be sent into prisons, so they are able to be sold on catalogues and order forms to prisoners, which is a proven money maker. Little did Celiane know, that when her pictures arrived and became popular as 'compound pictures' as they are called on the prison yards in the BOP, that prisoners nationwide would be instantly 'gunning her down', or what the prisoners called masturbating to the pictures. Celiane would be the paper target and there will be hundreds of thousands of prisoners masturbating to these images of her for years and years to come. Her pictures taken today would be bent and faded by the time Celiane's images were outdated and no longer clear enough to gun down.

When Celiane finally finished the set, Sweets, took her hand and led her to the bed room that was the faux wardrobe room, leading her into a new existence.

Things would never be the same for her after this day-after these experiences. Never again. She is a woman now. No longer a little girl. She has grown up and grabbed the bull by the horns and taken control of her life ... or so she had thought on that day.

PART II

Wicks & Shelby

On The Scene

fiat justitia, ruat caelun **(Latin):**

justice be done though the heavens fall

Chapter Ten

Six Months Later

They've argued for two months about it. Josue simply being hardheaded and adamant about not involving the police. He felt that by even calling the cops, that it would cause the immigration agents to immediately descend upon them and take their family away, only to deport them right back to Haiti, where the current regime-which was worse than the former one-would almost certainly label them as traitors to their country and have them immediately executed publicly. Things are bad in Haiti, even in these modern times. Josue couldn't stand for the American authorities to break up his family anymore than it already was. He faithfully watches the slanted CNN commentary, so he knows they would immediately send them to Chrome Detention Center in South Miami, the immigration holdover on Chrome Avenue, where people waited long periods of time to be deported. He also knew they would separate his whole family from each other. He sees it all the time on CNN and knows it is a thing.

Micheala was completely alone and desolate. She felt helpless and she just so very desperately wanted to go and get help from her twin brother, Michel. He would know exactly what to do in this situation, as he would in any dire circumstances. He had always had his own connections in the underground world. Even back in Port Au Prince while growing up, Michel had always found ways around the laws and ways to get things done. He was the one who had been able to get their, as yet to develop, family moved here to America illegally in the first place. But now they were suffering for it because they now can't go to the police for help. Josue was right about that, she knew that now. They would almost surely arrest and detain them. But she didn't agree that they shouldn't ask her brother Michel to help them with this very important family emergency. She just didn't understand why Josue, and his outdated sense of duty and responsibility would not accept Michel's help, after all, he was the only family they actually had here in America.

"What is the meaning of all of these, Micheala?" asked Josue heatedly. "Do you not think me man enough to take care of and protect our family? We don't need your brother to butt his head into our family affairs! I will take care of this myself. I know where this place is, this "Relax" place! I will take JonJon with me and I bring our Celiane home! I need no help from Michel! I am a man, Micheala!" With that said, he heatedly left the house in a storm of slammed doors and angry parting words.

That had been about a week and a half ago. Now, as a result of those actions, her husband was shot, JonJon and another Zoe Pound Member were dead, and she was all alone in this. She is without her husband. Her daughter is missing-and now facing the reality of having to raise her three sons all on her own was a completely daunting task. She was absolutely heartbroken and lost. She didn't know what to do and could barely think straight. Until she finally had decided to do what she had been begging Josue to do from the moment she had realized that they really couldn't call the police. She decided that she would call her twin, Michel. She decided to seek some real help. Some family help.

The police had come to her house about a week ago, the day after Josue had stormed out in a fit of anger after their argument-carrying his .38-caliber 'Saturday Night Special' revolver. They explained that there had been an altercation at a local massage parlor called Relax, in which her husband Josue, and two Zoe Pound Members had, according to their 'training and experience', apparently, tried to rob the place. The owner had been shot and killed, but not before shooting her husband and killing his two friends that had gone there with him. Now, Josue, being the only survivor, was being charged with the death of not only the parlor owner, who was also a gang member of the Black P-Stones, but also for the deaths of his own Zoe Pound friends in accordance with Florida's state law, along with 10-20-Life.

Florida law, under this subsection states that, once a felony murder is committed by one person, and other deaths results in commission of that crime, the one responsible for that murder shall also be held accountable for any other deaths as a result of the committed, no matter the actual cause of death. So, now that the .38 bullets that Josue had been firing were recovered from the owner's body, and the owners .40-caliber hollow points had been extracted from Josue and his two cohorts, his fate was almost surely sealed. He was going to be charged with all three bodies-as well as the 'use of the gun resulting in death', under Florida's notorious 10-

20-Life laws. Josue was looking at all PBLs, or punishable by life sentences for each charge and he still hadn't found out what he had even gone there for in the first place place: his daughter-Celiane's whereabouts.

Micheala had tried her hardest to explain to the xenophobic detectives that the men had only went there to confront the men who were pimping out her daughter, and had been trying to bring Celiane home to her family. But the soulless police could care less. Her cries and pleas all fell on deaf ears. A Haitian family's struggles isn't that glamorous to police. They didn't care. All that they did seem to care about-all they asked about, was hers or the men's affiliations to any Haitian gangs, and if there was a current war going on between the Black P-Stones and Zoe Pound or even with Haitian Sensations, since they most definitely knew about her twin, Michel, and his being a lieutenant in the Haitian Sensations drug cartel.

After so much of their constant badgering, and her pleas going ignored, she had most definitely had enough of their nonsense and with an angry finality, she put all of them out of her house and out of her life. Unfortunately, they were now also out of Celiane's life as well, so they wouldn't be helping to find her either. It was a lose-lose situation all around and she felt like nothing that she could do would help. She didn't know what to do or how to help. When she had wanted to involve Michel, Josue had vetoed that idea, so now what? she had asked herself.

Before answering, she decided to go and visit Josue at Gun

Club, Palm Beach County's main county jail. She was led to a glass window in a little booth and told to wait. The only reason she was allowed into Gun Club on the second floor for a visit was because Josue was in the jail hospital and couldn't access the video visits screen on that floor like the rest of the jail. It was a good thing too, since he would have given the prosecution enough evidence to bury himself if it had been on a regular recorded video visit, as he didn't know about keeping one's mouth shut while inside of any jail or prison situation and how his own words could be later used against him.

"Oh! My goodness! Josue, are you okay?" asked Micheala incredulously, eyes immediately starting to water up at seeing the condition that he was in. He had bandages all around his left arm and he was all wrapped up around his ribs where one of the bullets had penetrated and had broken his lowest left rib, only inches away from his vital organs.

"Oh, hush, woman. I am fine. I am more hurt by the fact that I have failed you and our daughter by not bringing her home." He lowered his head. "I have shamed our family and proved that I was wrong in not allowing you to involve Michel. I should have accepted the offer of his help and brought honor to our family, but instead, I have shamed us all. I now have to ask my brother-in-law to bring honor by bringing home our daughter and completing the task I have failed at. I am sorry, my wife ... "

"It is okay, husband. We will get her back, I promise ... " Micheala had said.

115

§§§§

Once Micheala finished visiting Josue, she made it home where she relieved the next door neighbor from watching her boys and proceeded to cry alone and her oldest son, 12 year old Marquis, came worriedly knocking at her door, bringing her a glass of water and checking on her.

"It's okay, mama. Everything is gonna be okay. I love you mama ... " said Marquis, closing her door behind him. His maturity and tenderness touching her while making her cry even more. She began to panic. How could she do this all by herself? Now she had not only lost her daughter, who had always helped to take care of her three brothers, but now, she had lost her husband as well. She couldn't provide for her whole household without her daughter and husband. Now she would also have to send him money for commissary and hire him an attorney. She had no idea how she would or even if she could do any of it. She definitely couldn't do it alone. She has no choice but to call her twin and ask for his help. She picked up her phone, her decision having finally been made.

A half an hour later, Michel was sitting in her kitchen, while his partner in crime, Lucretia, played basketball with the boys at the nearby park, giving Micheala a chance to update him as to everything that was going on with their family, starting her story with everything that had happened back from around 6 months ago. That was when Celiane had began to change. She had met some boy with a big fancy car. A big car that looked way too expensive for a young boy Celiane's age to be driving. The night Micheala saw him, Celiane hadn't seen her mother taking the trash out, when the boy had dropped her off a few houses down, proving that she had been trying to keep him a secret, knowing that she and Josue would never approve.

"What did this car look like, sister?" asked Michel, as they were conversing in Creole, their native language.

"It was a big, green convertible and had really big white truck wheels, where it is sitting up high, like a truck. But brother, it is not a truck, it is a car. I saw one like it once on a Trick Daddy music video that Marquis was watching. I know-" She began to ramble on, but her twin stopped her, interrupting.

"Okay, sister. Not to worry. I know just who to call," he said decisively, already scrolling through his phone, stopping at the name, Wicks.

Wicks would definitely help him after all they had just been through together with that whole gang war with the Mexican cartel, thought Michel.

.. it had been just about a year ago, his Haitian Sensations colleague, Steff, had called he and Lucretia, known as Crea, to come deal with some problem with a competing Mexican organization-the Gulf Cartel, based in Matamoros, Tamualipas. Mexico's most Northeastern corner state. It had all started at a local Youth Center, where Wicks had been volunteering at and had spread out from there.

After two high ranking members of Haitian Sensations had disappeared with blame falling on the Gulf Cartel, some of their own Haitian Sensations kids-who weren't even a part of their organization yet, only prospecting-had attacked and killed some of the Gulf Cartel's kids in a teen night club called Chance's and it ended up in a blaze that had subsequently killed over a dozen kids and hospitalizing many more with serious bodily injuries, gaining bad publicity for both cartels with national coverage.

It became a tit-for-tat situation with casualties on both sides-until finally the kettle boiled over where both sides participated in a full on gang war while on the 'jit' floor, at Gun Club Main Jail in West Palm Beach, right next to the Palm Beach International Airport.

Michel and Crea worked behind the scenes with Haitian Sensations new shot caller; Antoine Jean, to complete the transfer of power from the old leader, Big Head, and ultimately squash the beef with the Gulf Cartel, whose second in command had been plotting a coup with Big Head the entire time, actually starting the whole beef in the first place, trying to take over the already quite powerful cartel.

Ultimately though, Wicks and Leo, another Haitian Sensations lieutenant, actually went to the Gun Club County Jail-along with the Gulf Cartel's representatives, and they had a meeting with the kids on their respective sides and were able to negotiate a truce between both factions.

Meanwhile, Crea and Steff-along with Michel backing them up-had eliminated Big Head's closest allies that might have bucked about the decapitation of Big Head and Antoine Jean's silent takeover of the Haitian Sensations drug cartel, some of whom were involved with the notorious 400 Mawazo Haitian gang operating out of Port Au Prince.

All in all, Wicks had been at the center of the whole truce between Haitian Sensations and the Gulf Cartel, but it had ultimately got rid of Big Head's tyranny and firmly placed Antoine Jean at the helm of Haitian Sensations, while his protege Buju, had taken the helm of the 400 Mawazo. The outcome had been what was best for all of those concerned since then, because the new relationship between Haitian Sensations and Gulf Cartel-and specifically the Felix Family-had allowed them to control the trade market value of fentanyl, cocaine, flaka, and heroin. Without under cutting each other and having agreed on an inflated base drug price for kilograms, they had effectively monopolized the entire drug trade's markets in the South Eastern United States.

They had killed two birds with one stone while simultaneously helping Wicks with his Youth Center problems. This gave Michel the confidence that he could now seek a helping hand from Wicks where he himself would most certainly be under a high level of scrutiny and suspicion of being responsible for any bodies being dropped for those pimping out his precious niece while retrieving her and bringing her safely home. Wicks, on the contrary, would be under no suspicion, him lacking the prerequisite connection to his family or his organization. For this reason, Michel felt reassured.

He looked down at his Samsung Galaxy S, seeing Wicks' name and number on the screen, a number that he thought that he would never have to dial. But dire circumstances call for drastic measures. His decision was finally made.

Michel pressed send ... and by doing so, he set a whole chain of events into action. As hard of a decision that it was to make, it was one that he would never regret.

Chapter Eleven

Wicks was outside of the Red Roof Inn up in North Palm Beach County the day that he missed Michel's call. He was using his Sony Cybershot and was recording, as there was a grey Mercedez C-Class pulling up, confirming his suspicions. He continued to record as a brunette, white or hispanic woman in a business pantsuit with tan skin and pretty features, and a lot of curves in all of the right places, came out to meet the man in the Benz and shook his hand with an all business expression on her beautiful face. He indicated the rear of the car and they walked over to the trunk as he hit the button on the key fob to pop the trunk. He then grabbed two, as she grabbed one of the file boxes that were revealed in the open trunk space and she closed the trunk, leading him up to her room on the second floor.

It hadn't been such a difficult case to figure out for Wicks. Especially since he was a federally convicted felon, and the opportunities for work at his private investigations firm hadn't exactly been beating down the door for him, leaving him with a lot of thinking time. He had actually gotten lucky and a friend of a friend's father was having some problems at his small law office on 9th and Dixie Highway in Lake Worth, the Law Offices of Charles Kline, ESQ. They thought that maybe Wicks could contribute some help.

Attorney Charles Kline has a nice little boutique law office for divorce, immigration, and workers comp-type claims. He also does

121

some random civil claims or any other miscellaneous things to help clients, or the friends and family of clients. Wicks was not Mr. Kline's first choice for an investigator. Actually, Mr. Kline already had his own in-house investigator who he uses for all of his cases, but here he was, unable to do that in this case, because if he-meaning his investigator-was part of the conspiracy, then Mr. Kline would never know, as the guy certainly wouldn't expose himself. Thus, Mr. Kline's requirement of some outside help.

That in turn, created an opportunity for Jean 'Wicks' Pierre, and Pierre Investigative Services, Inc., to find out who is behind the missing records, and if the partner, Craig Green, and investigator for Mr. Kline's law firm, Alex Boatman, were involved with the theft-and everyone agreed that they were involved-Pierre Investigative Services, Inc. would have their first law firm as a client. That is, if Wicks could get the proof of their involvement, which he would certainly do.

With Mr. Kline's law firm, would come plenty of work, which they needed, since they had only been open for two months and had only landed a couple online skip traces for vehicle repossessions, which didn't really bring home the bacon, so to speak. Luckily, Shelby, Jean's girlfriend, was still working, and as a cop of cops at that. An unlikely couple, felon and cop. He guessed she 'felon' love. He laughed at the prisoner humor ironically.

Shelby wasn't any ordinary cop though. She is IAD, or Internal Affairs Division and her job was to police the police. She had been a Palm Beach Sheriff's Office homicide detective until she had shot her own partner, just as he had been trying, and had almost shot an unarmed black kid in the Whitehouse projects. Now, she specializes in investigating officer involved shootings, as well as corruption in the police department all over Palm Beach County. In only six months, she had placed 11 cops behind bars, and she said she was only just getting started. She had always wanted to make right all of the injustice in the world, starting with Palm Beach County. Ignoring all of the cliches, she wants to make a difference, to leave the world a better place than when she came into it.

Really, Shelby wasn't getting too involved in the private investigations business that Jean had started, as she had a job where she felt like she could make a difference, make her community a better place, and she also wanted her man, Wicks, or Jean, depending on the situation because he has dual personality disorder, to have something of his own to make a difference in his own right, and to have some semblance of being prosperous, productive and helpful in his work. She and Mr. Kline had pulled some strings to get into court with a petition to expunge his record, in order to let him start anew and build his business up on his own hard work, but they were still waiting on that one. The judge was known to be tough, but he was also known to be a fair judge as well.

They were all really counting on the motion being granted, but in this same judicial system that had originally made Wicks "A Victim of Justice", the new term commonly used to describe those who are victimized by systemic injustice, there was never a way to predict an outcome of any motion. Much less any motion filed by Wicks.

Thus far in his current investigations into Mr. Kline's missing client files, it was looking as if all of the missing files were for Mr. Kline's clients that had actually lost their cases and had already been deported. There were also several workers comp case files missing as well, but those were limited to those who had died as a result of their injuries and their families were the ones seeking victim or workers compensation proceedings.

At first, Wicks had started by following the partner and other investigator, and he had discovered that both would always show up here, at the Red Roof Inn, North of West Palm Beach. Both met separately with this same lady. Susan Parker was the generic name that the license plate came back to when he asked Shelby to run the tag on the white Tesla for him on her IAD computer system. It was good to have connections like that, he laughed to himself at the humor of it. Him, an ex-convict, in a live-in relationship with the cop of all cops, while also working as a private investigator. There wasn't that much irony in the whole wide world, was there?

The lady had no record. Not even any traffic infractions or citations. She was clean as hell. It didn't make sense at first. The missing documents. They were almost all immigrants. Mostly Mexican or Guatemalan, Central American, but mixed in with some Caribbean as well. This is where he started, with the court's docket sheets. From there he got a hold of some of the hearing

124

minutes that had been transcribed for appeal purposes through Mr. Kline's clerk of court accounts. From there he was able to go to the clerk's office and pay for print out duplicates of at least all of the transcripts of the missing files of Mr. Kline's clients. From there he spent days and nights dissecting the files to compare them and find a commonality they all might have. At first he couldn't, besides the fact of them all having been losing deportation cases, or workers comp cases that had resulted in death.

He decided to try a different tact. What of possible value could be in any of these old closed case files? It would have to be valuable enough to get a junior partner and respected investigator involved in the theft conspiracy. Only one thing in these files could be valuable, and it wasn't about the cases. Not case law. Jean had to really contemplate. The most popular crime in South Florida now, well after drugs of course, was credit card fraud. And what did one need to get a credit card?

To get a credit card, you would need a name, of course. A social security number? An address to send it to? That would be it basically. So, each one of the people with the missing files had been here on a student visa, or basically had just been here to go to school, so their social security cards all had the "school use only" or the "not for work use" disclaimers printed on the cards. They are also known as dreamers.

Jean had finally figured it out. It had hit him, just like that. It was the reason she was using the Red Roof Inn, it is perfect for her purposes, one main address with an endless amount of room numbers and no mail boxes for each room, all mail would go to the front desk. The guy who worked day shift on weekdays when mail ran at the front desk would definitely be in on it. He would have to be actually.

He started to go deeper into the closed case files. Almost all of these people that were deported had either caught a charge for a domestic, DUI, or petty theft and pleaded guilty, then later on had allowed their visa to expire, hence the discovery of the violation of their school visa. All the others, had caught felonies, and that in itself would automatically subject them to a deportation hearing upon a guilty plea or verdict.

Once these people were deported, coming back, or 're-entry' as it was called, is a federal crime, so most of them don't even take the chance coming back, at which point their social security numbers are just sitting there without use. Some of them might have financed cars or payed telephone bills, among other things, but most don't even have a credit score and even if they had bad credit, they would still probably be approved for credit cards or loans, everyone deserving a second chance and all of that mess .

This is an incredible racket that they had tapped into and Wicks could see what was really going on here. But it still didn't explain how they were using the credit cards on such a massive scale as they would have to be in order to turn a lawyer and a good investigator. Wicks would find out though. This guy was his competition and he was dirty. Dirty like Wicks' ex-criminal lawyer, long departed, and those DEA and ATF task force agents, long ago indicted, that had set him up on trumped-up padded charges all of those years ago. He had no patience, respect or sympathy for those who would abuse their positions of power or authority to oppress the 'lower society' so he would enjoy taking them all down.

Alex Boatman left the motel room and as Wicks continued on with his surveillance, he got back into his C-Class and backed out and quickly drove out the parking lot. Wicks got behind him, staying two cars back. He followed the investigator back to Okeechobee Boulevard, where he pulled into the parking lot on the side of Cheetahs of Palm Beach, a popular strip club that caters to rich guys and drug dealers. A girl came out of the back door and immediately got into the passenger seat. From where he was parked, Wicks couldn't see any real details about the girl, but by observing her skimpy attire, he would say that she was definitely a stripper, quite possibly with a name like Candi, Mandi, or even Brandi. Definitely one of those, yet ending with an 'I'. Then, there is also the fact that her head immediately went down into Alex Boatman's lap upon entering the car, giving him another definitive clue.

Since he has a dash-cam set up and is recording all of his driving movements for possible law suits or law enforcement set ups, while following his subject, Wicks only had pulled back out the Sony Cybershot camera when he had parked, so he was recording all of this previously going down on his camera. Wicks had installed hidden cameras at Kline's law office, so he already had the evidence of the theft of three file boxes. But now, he believed that catching Boatman and his co-conspirator in the exchange of the case files at the Red Roof Inn in addition, was plenty to prove their involvement and to get Wicks the full time position as Mr. Kline's new permanent in-house investigator. That was his main goal: to have some reliable and constant work coming in to sustain his brand new business.

So, having enough to show Mr. Kline, he now wanted to satisfy his own curiosity and interview Boatman himself to find out what this scam was truly about and how he even got involved in it in the first place. Wicks had to know what was really behind it all ... and he would.

Chapter Twelve

After Wicks ended up pulling a 'Cheaters' move, rolling up on Boatman all fast with his camera rolling, busting him in the middle of his little tricking session, and scaring away Mandy, it had been Mandy with a 'Y' after all, Wicks had him right where he wanted him: Busted, disgusted, and never to be trusted. If Boatman didn't want this filmed trick session to make it to his wife, he knew exactly what Wicks wanted from him, and right now, that is the truth.

"So, tell me what she is and how it works," says Wicks to a shaking Boatman.

"Man, I can't talk about it! They will know, they'll kill me and-"

"Mother fucker, I'll fucking kill you!" interrupted Wicks, as he backhand slapped him to show he's dead serious.

"Come on, man! I can't!" he whimpered, begging Wicks with everything in his being for Wicks not to force him to talk. The seriousness in Wicks tattooed face belied his intention of getting to the bottom of the whole scheme, and he knew that it runs very deep. Wicks slapped the shit out of him again. Ironically, the man's pale face was now turning pink. This very street smart investigator, who for many years, used to be a street cop up in Chester, Pennsylvania, had started to cry, and begged with his eyes. But Wicks felt no empathy. He had done extensive research on Alex Boatman, even more than the regular background check that Mr. Kline's office had done on him when they hired him as their private investigator full time. What Wicks had come up with was that, Chester's Police Department had pretty much forced him into early retirement amid accusations of corruption; excessive force; and the shooting of an unarmed black man in front of his 11 year old son.

Wicks had absolutely no sympathy for Boatman's dirty ass, and he didn't have any problem ending Alex Boatman's miserable life, just as he had ended the unarmed and innocent black man's life that he had killed without reason or remorse. Even on top of that, he had been represented by the union in Chester and had won three quarters pay for the rest of his life for retirement. His pension. He had abused the justice system, taken payouts, killed, and abused those he was charged with protecting and serving. This was one of the main problems with the criminal justice system. Those charged with upholding the law were, most of the time, breaking it and thinking themselves above it. Wicks and his girl, Shelby Nash, had charged themselves with bringing forth some justice. Real justice. A kind of street justice.

"Uhh-huh. I'm starting to lose patience ... " was all Wicks said, after delivering another blinding slap to his face.

"Okay! Okay, man! Just please keep me out of it! It's Lexi Marley! That's who I've been giving the files to! She's using the names and social security numbers of deported aliens to do shit, rent houses and pay off insurance policies and loans! A lot of other shit too! Please man! Just let me go!" he cried.

130

"You're saying that it was Lexi Gambini?! From the Gambini crime family?" Wicks asked, incredulously.

"I'm saying that it doesn't matter anyway, because she will have us both fucking killed man, whoever the fuck you are, and whoever the fuck you work for, this is some next level shit, this shit is some smoke you don't want, trust me," the ex-cop spat, literally scared to death. It was all for nothing though, as Wicks was well aware of whom Lexi Gambini-Marley is, as well as what her family was capable of, Wicks could care less. There wasn't a man that breathes the same air as him that can instill fear inside of Wicks. Those who went against him were already long ago turned into worm food as a result.

In the last two years, he had been through more than most gangstas see in their entire lives. Back in 2008 he had been set up by some dirty DEA/ATF Task Force agents, over-charged and over-sentenced when he not only refused to cooperate with them, but also spit in the face of the prosecutor asking him to rat. He was subsequently overcharged with stacked 924(c) counts and sentenced to a minimum mandatory sentence of 66 years consecutively in a Maximum Security United States Penitentiary in retaliation for his actions. Then, in 2020, he got away with murder while at USP Canaan in Pennsylvania. Shortly after that, in 2021, he was finally released when a federal investigation was initiated into those same dirty DEA/ATF Task Force agents which provided a favorable outcome for Wicks: They were all indicted, prosecuted, and sentenced for corruption, having padded cases to get lengthy sentences for people not deserving of them, as well as the murder of an unarmed black man in front of his aging mother. Many cases were over-turned any instance where those same dirty agents were involved. Wicks' case happened to be one of them, and fortunately for him, he was granted immediate release and freed. He vowed never to become a 'Victim of Justice' again, and with his girlfriend Shelby, they were dedicated to helping to prevent anyone else from becoming victims of justice, and had gotten off to a hell of a start.

When Wicks and Shelby had met helping kids at a local Youth Center, Shelby had hipped Wicks up to some prospective Haitian Sensations kids selling drugs from inside the Youth Center. In the midst of all of that, when Wicks' baby nephew, 11 year old Lil Ray, is shot by another kid near the Youth Center, Wicks is forced to make some moves on the opposition cartel, intending to frame Haitian Sensations for the Matamoros, Gulf Cartel's ranking members getting murdered, as well as the staging of the suspected robbery of millions of dollars in cash from the Gulf Cartel's cash strong hold and the attack of La Taqueria.

The Gulf Cartel's second in command, Iggy, had then tried to hire some mercenaries to kidnap the boss' favorite niece, Liz, who is also unknowingly dating Wicks' oldest nephew, EJ. Wicks, EJ and Liz ended up killing all four of the mercenaries, then they tracked the attempted attack back to the second in command's brutal cousin who was the one that had hired them. Then they figured out from there about Iggy's ultimate betrayal by his involvement. Liz ended up cutting Iggy's head off of his body for his treachery in order to make an example of him and then the Gulf Cartel boss had them run over his head with a stretch Hummer limousine, smashing the heads like smashing pumpkins. Wicks ended up brokering a peace treaty between the factions, but then again, all he had simply wanted was for them to keep the drugs and gang banging away from the kids at the Youth Center.

So, after all that he had been through, figuring this scam out was like nothing to him.

§§§§

It was the most complicated, yet interesting scam that Wicks had ever seen. It was like a Ponzi scheme, yet also like a pyramid scheme as well. It was the scheme that would help the mob to, not only launder their illegal funds, but to also reinvest them into legal ventures through shell companies to have the money be able to come back into their other shell companies and make them profit. All off of the backs of illegal immigrants and their temporary social security numbers that they couldn't protest or even find out about. Who would have ever thought? They would forever be in the dark. If they did come and trespass back on American soil, they were committing a federal crime just by doing so, and so who could they complain to about it?

Their social security numbers were being used and built upon. The names and numbers were being used in a three-card-monty type of scheme. First, the money, a dirty $9,000 dollars, was being deposited into bank accounts of the name that they were using at that time. Then a secured loan would be taken out against that account balance, which the bank would always approve because there was no risk involved being that the money that was being borrowed against was still sitting inside of the account held by that bank. So, they would then take that loan and deposit it into an account at a new bank, then borrow the same against that account. That loan would then be used to open a third account at a third bank, and the same would be done again, using that third money to pay back the loan at the first bank. This process, called boosting, would then skyrocket the credit report numbers. It would actually look like they had payed off three hefty loans, when in fact they had only payed interest on those loans. They just used the same deposit three different times to move it around and pay off the other loans. In doing this, they were not only defrauding the banks, but also the three major credit report companies. They were basically getting a high credit report in less than three months, saying that they had payed off the whole amounts of three different loans, when all they did was pay the bank's interest on the loaned money. Being that they were secured loans, the interest would never be too high.

Then, with the incredibly high credit scores-all off of those same names and social security numbers would begin to take out larger unsecured loans-to 'invest' into any of the Gambini Family legal businesses. Then the Gambini Family would pay off these

134

loans with all dirty money, sometimes $20,000 or $30,000 at a time.

Now usually, IRS notifications are legally required when depositing anything over $10,000 from any of the financial institutions, but not when paying off a loan. No IRS notification is necessary when large loans are payed off. So, basically the Gambini Family found a legal way to get around the risk in money laundering. That wasn't all though.

It had all come out when Wicks had interviewed the lawyer and investigator that worked at Mr. Kline's office. They both told all when Wicks ended up putting the pressure on them to talk. It all led back to the Gambini Family. Their monies were being deposited into their own shell companies when the interest was payed off. So they now had clean money along with the high credit scores of the identities that they themselves had created. Those identities could now be used to not only donate money to Big Louie Gambini's campaign for Mayor of West Palm Beach, because of the $1,000 dollar cap that is now imposed on all campaign contributions after the whole Trump Stolen Election campaign scam. But they could also be used for further fraudulent activities, some of which included them using the credit cards to rent luxuries such as Lamborghinis and mansions for the future mayor on turo.com and the airbnb.com for the up and coming election campaign. There were many other uses for the monies that they would get through the credit cards of all those illegal immigrants. Then there was the best part of it which for them is, if they did even ever come back to the States, they could never use their own social security numbers again or risk being charged federally and deported all over again. It was a hell of a scheme, was what Wicks sat there thinking to himself, now what to do with this important information was his next problem. If he led Mr. Kline down this path, it could very well be trouble for Mr. Kline and as his new employer, that is not what Wicks wants for him. Maybe he can give him the bare minimum and deal with the repercussions himself, if it ever even comes to that.

Wicks had already convinced the attorney and the investigator that it was in their best interests to get ghost and find another life somewhere else. He didn't think that they would have too much trouble, he was sure that the Gambini Family weren't only blackmailing them, they were sure to have nest eggs set up for themselves. So, now with them out of the picture, Wicks could get the full time job as Mr. Kline's investigator, and that was all of the help that Wicks needed. That was his fresh start. His new life.

That was all, until he had finally noticed Michel's missed call. He knew that it would be something very important if Michel was calling in his marker after only a year having passed since Wicks had given it to him. Then, once he had retrieved the call and listening to the problem, and having found out what was needed of him, his priorities immediately changed. Celiane was now his new top priority, he decided. He would wrap up this Gambini Family business quickly and move on to locating and bringing this 16 year old girl home, and then work on helping her father-who had only been trying to protect his family and save his daughter. This is the kind of case that he had founded Pierre Investigative Services for: To make a difference and help those who could not get help from the police or system.

Wicks has his own system. A street system. He played judge, jury, and executioner when warranted. 'Welcome to street justice by Wicks', the sign should say.

Chapter Thirteen

IAD Detective Shelby Nash smiled to herself. She never knew that she could love anything more than being an investigator, but within the last year, or is it a year and a half? she asks herself before continuing in her thoughts ... well, since then, she has found two things more important: Wicks, her live-in boyfriend; and the Youth Center that they both volunteer at, teaching these kids in her new Explorers Program, specifically for kids at the Youth Center, who are interested in criminal investigations and law enforcement careers. There were even a few kids who had expressed an interest in forensics. She was talking to a friend at DNA International Labs in Boca Raton, to come in twice a month and give classes on crime scene investigations and the forensics side of criminal investigations.

She had first submitted an idea to teach girls wanting to learn and train for a future career in Law Enforcement, but the county had ended up stepping up over the city for funding of her program, on the specific condition that it be a gender neutral program, which was the newest politically correct and trendy thing. Well, all was good with Shelby as long as her program was actually helping. Really making a difference. Her wanting to leave this world a better place than when she came into it was something that she was very passionate about and always pursued. That was the reason that her own career had evolved in the way that it had.

It had all started about a year ago, after Shelby had shot a

PBSO Homicide Detective who had been about to shoot an unarmed 14 year old African-American kid in the White House project housing park, while they had been investigating a ZMF gang member's murder. A split second before Mike Chambers had pulled his trigger, Shelby had pulled hers, sending a jacketed .40-caliber into Mike Chambers' vest, knocking him off of his feet and simultaneously saving Jovan Mills 14 year old life. It had ultimately marked an end for Shelby's career with Palm Beach Sheriff's Office, and also introduced her to her new career at IAD, or the Internal Affairs Division. An investigator at IAD had recognized the courage that it must have taken to shoot her own senior partner for some poor black kid from the projects, regardless of knowing that he had been wearing a vest and placing her shot accordingly.

"What about pinging his cell phone location off of the cell tower?" asked L'Tesha Smith, Shelby's favorite Explorer, bringing her back from her thoughts.

"Remember, the disappearance happened in 1997, so this was before this kind of technology existed, but very good thinking. That is the newest investigative technique that we have available to us now. It has made an amazing difference in investigations recently. So, good thinking, L'Tesha, looks like somebody's been watching CSI on television. Okay guys, I'll see you on Tuesday, have a wonderful weekend ... " said Shelby, dismissing her class of Explorers. They had been working on an old case, one that was solved, but one in which facts were available for her to use. She then would give the kids what the investigators had had on the first day of the investigation and would see if they would follow along the same steps or clues, taking the same path as the original investigators did, or if they would come up with an even better idea or clue. It was good practice, and because the cases were already solved, she could point out things that they might have missed, things they wouldn't miss, next time.

Things were actually going so great that she was going to start bringing some live cold cases to them next. These were OUS cases, or open/unsolved cases, so real cases, with a real killer still out there. She had to go through a lot of yellow tape to get these approved, and also, she had compromised on redacted versions of the real case files, or files with all of the names deleted from them.

"Hey, Miss Shelby, how are ya?" asked 'Lil Fade, one of the boxers and basketball players that was trained by either her boyfriend Jean, or his alter ego, Wicks, depending on the situation. Fade had actually been the one who had shot 'Lil Ray-Wicks' baby nephew-three times and had almost lost his own life for that. But after getting jumped while in Gun Club County Jail, causing a major concussion and brain swelling, in which an emergency medical procedure had to be performed at the jail to save his life, he had made a complete turn-around, becoming a completely different kid. Now, he actually trained 'Lil Ray, who now looked up to him, and Wicks trained them both. It was Wicks' words and influence that had ultimately reached Fade and many other Haitian Sensations members and encouraged them to make the change before ending up like he had with a 66 year sentence inside of a Maximum Security Federal Penitentiary. He had made a difference in these kids lives and now Shelby also wanted to do the same, hence, her offering to teach the Explorers Program.

"Oh, hey. You training here tonight?" Shelby asked, smiling at him. She was very proud of the changes and sacrifices that he had been making lately, and always took time to reassure and encourage him to stay on the right path, her biggest fear being afraid of losing even one of these kids.

"Yea, but we done already. I just wanted to say 'good job' with that Jones arrest that you made. It's about time that someone got that dirty mo-" Fade started.

"Watch your mouth! What did I tell you about that?" asked Shelby, interrupting him.

"To watch my mouth in front of the ladies. I know! I'm sorry ..."

"It's okay. So, I take it that you've had a run in with Jones before?" asked Shelby.

"Hell yea! He beat my-Oh, sorry! I mean yes, he arrested me once and he broke my nose. Well, I'm glad that he finally got caught. So, I'll see ya later, Miss Shelby!" and with that, 'Lil Fade took off back towards the locker room to take a shower.

§§§§

After receiving a text from Wicks to meet her at the Law Offices of Charles F. Kline, she left the Youth Center up on 45th street and drove the 10 minute drive to 9th and Dixie in downtown Lake Worth. After the whole ordeal with Mr. Kline's partner and investigator's disappearance, Wicks had been given the exclusive account with his firm. So, he now had his own office in the upstairs apartment of Mr. Kline's law office. When Wicks had explained about the theft of those files from the law office and said that he didn't know who they had been bringing the files to, Mr. Kline, being an extremely smart individual, didn't push. He read between the lines that it would be best left alone.

Wicks wanted to keep the Gambini Family involvement to himself, not only for Mr. Kline's protection, but also in case he ever needed a favor one day. So, he stored his photos and interview tapes of Alex Boatman and Craig Green in his safe in Shelby and his condo at the Moorings of Lantana.

When Shelby walked into the office, there was a Haitian man and woman sitting at Mr. Kline's desk. The man looked serious, the woman, crying. They looked alike and she came to find out that they were twins and not husband and wife as she had originally thought. Jean had been waiting for her by Mr. Kline's door.

"I'm so sorry, ma'am. I just don't represent anyone in criminal court. I don't think you understand. I'm a divorce lawyer, I'm not qualified to go to misdemeanor court, much less represent on a triple murder rap. Now, I can recommend Michael G. Smith out of Ft. Lauderdale. He is the best criminal defense lawyer in South Florida. I can speak to him for you and-"

"No!" said Michel, interrupting Mr. Kline's attempt to convince him of his inability to properly represent Micheala's husband, Josue. "We not trust wit nobody else but man who gave Wicks good job! We want fa you fa represent me broda, Josue," added Michel emotionally, his Creole accent becoming more prominent with his emotions.

Mr. Kline looked at Jean and Shelby, who were now standing by the entrance, his eyes begging them to help explain his position to them, the impossibility of him representing on this kind of case, but they could see that it would be a fruitless endeavor to change Michel's mind once it had been made up.

"I guess it's time to brush up on criminal law, Mr. Kline," said Jean, smiling at the irony of Mr. Kline's predicament. "Michel, Micheala, would you follow Shelby and I upstairs, we can discuss our other piece of business in private ... " He led the way.

Once they were seated and able to discuss the other matter in private, Michel sat and poured a drink, then explained how they had come to find themselves in the situation that they were in to Shelby and Wicks, as well as why Josue was sitting in Gun Club County Jail with three PBL capital murder charges and an armed home invasion count, even though there was no home involved. It had been a jack shack, and a dirty one at that if they had underage girls working inside of there, as they had been found to have had upon further investigation.

Shelby led Micheala to the kitchenette to get her some coffee

143

and to allow Michel to give Wicks all of the intricate details of how his niece came to be getting pimped, starting with the modeling gigs and ending with her doing porn and then 'private porn' in which basically some old man was paying for the pussy and a lot of times there were trains being ran and some very weird and eccentric acts being performed on her. Ultimately, she ended up selling her body at Relax, as well as having taken on clients from her OnlyFans and InstaGram pages for money.

When they had looked all of her socials up, as well as her work on PornHub and her Sugarbaby.com listing, they saw that she was being pushed by her womanager, Sweets. They tried to get a location from any of her pictures or posts, however, that location option was blocked or turned off.

"The locals have been all over Haitian Sensations and Zoe Pound since that shit went down. Dem 'tink we at war with some P-Stones or me handle it myself wit my Haitian Sensation bruddas. I need to be on camera when ya go get Celiane or they will come fa me, " Michel said, to clarify why he needed Wicks help so bad, and this is why he was calling in his marker so fast.

"Okay, don't you worry about it, this is something we will handle, you do realize they still finna come at you for this with everything they got, right? On camera or not, they finna know you sent somebody, so from now on, no phone calls between us. When you do need to meet up or come here, leave your phone and don't drive a car with On-Star or any kind of GPS systems. They finna be on you, we don't want any attention on us. That's why I was adamant about Mr. Kline being your lawyer. Any other questions?" asked Wicks, finishing up.

"Tank ya, Wicks, me owe ya ... " said Michel, standing up and offering his hand for Wicks to shake. They shook up on it and Micheala left with him, still crying her eyes out, her heart broken and whole world turned upside down.

After they had gone, Shelby nodded her understanding in Wicks getting involved in what the ignorant and clueless police thought was another gang war. She would support and back him, come hell or high water. She also had a deeper understanding from a mother's perspective after hearing Micheala's side of the story and knowing that the only way that this pimp could have kept Celiane away from her family and from her little brothers that she adored, was he had her hooked on drugs. Molly was most common for this type of situation, but it might also be heroin. Either way, it would take a miracle to get Celiane back after she had been turned out, especially with a drug addiction on top of all of the emotional trauma that she had already been dealing with.

"How do you wanna handle it? Simple extraction?" asked Shelby, already down to go.

"I'm thinking so. We'll see, but I gotta find her first. I'ma have to get EJ to do some online recon, maybe set up a fake photoshoot or an escort appointment, I'll think of something, this is the type of shit I started the private investigations office for. Some people can't go to the police for help, so this is where we see if I can really make a difference for those who can't protect themselves. I'll get her back, her father almost lost his life trying to protect her and bring her home. I won't let that be in vain. I'll go and get her back, I can't let her fall to that type of life like that ... " Wicks said, trailing off.

"We ... " said Shelby.

"Huh?"

"I said 'we'. I mean we will get her back, We can't let her fall to the streets like that. You said 'I', so I corrected you, to 'we'," said Shelby simply.

"Are you sure you wanna get involved? I can handle this, Shel. Ain't no reason for you to have to risk it now that you're IAD. A lot of cops would love for you to get caught on the other side of the fence. You don't have to-" he started.

"I want to," she said, keeping it simple, interrupting him. "I gotta help where I can."

"Oh-kay ... I'll start the research and recon, just remember that we can't let them catch you involved in this with your pants down, that's what they would want ... " he replied.

"Baby, you're the only one who can catch me with my pants down ... " Shelby said, slowly walking up and kissing him on the mouth with desire.

"Well, baby, I would like to do some 'catching' right about now ... " Wicks answered, kissing her back with equal love and lust in his eyes.

They went into the other room in the office and did some

146

investigating of their own. But it had been initiated, a decision had been made and Shelby and Wicks were now on the case. One way or the other, they would bring Celiane home safely to her family, or what was left of her family, after her dad had been shot and arrested. Wicks is a man of focus. He is relentless in his pursuit or righteousness in completing his tasks. He just had taken on a task of all tasks and would most likely lose a lot before he won.

Chapter Fourteen

- One Month Later -

Things had been going great for about four months with Celiane and the 'Baby Steps' program that Sweets had been breaking her on. They *had* been going great, that is. Celiane had smoothly conformed to her role as his prime, but she was very unsettled about living in Thug Mansion with all of the other girls. She wasn't very vocal, but he had eyes, didn't he? He is very observant. He could see that she wasn't feeling it, hence, his next step: Roxys. He had her on molly for a few months, a bit of coke and flaka here and there, but then getting her on roxys was the next logical step of his plan of implementing her dependency, she would really rely on him then. So, he did that about two months ago and instead of better, things had actually began to get worse.

He had moved "Jolly" into Thug Mansion first. Jolly was the nickname he gave to Celiane's friend Nicky, for how she would pop a Jolly Rancher in her mouth and go to town on any dick placed in her path. Jolly was a real man eater. But that had been a bad move for Sweets, as Celiane quickly figured out that Jolly was trying and succeeding in getting a lot of attention from Sweets. Jealousy was a pimp's friend in some cases, as it could make his hoes work harder-compete more-but in other cases, it can also work against him, like it did in this case. Luckily, Jolly had already turned 18 last month, so when Celiane had sliced her face 'buck-fifty' style with a razor blade-boxcutter-and he had brought her around the corner to Wellington Regional Hospital, Child Protective Services couldn't get involved and wouldn't be called. Not that he was really worried about it since he was unaware that they had both been underage when he had met them.

Ever since that night, things had quickly went downhill for Sweets and his stable. Since Jolly's face looked almost Chucky-like, and then having closed the cut with 28 staples while leaving her with a permanent stomach curdling scar from her left eyebrow down to her chin, she could bring in no money more than maybe $20 blow jobs in bars and clubs where it was dark enough-and the men drunk enough-not to notice it all. So, she mainly kept the house for them, cooked, cleaned, and did laundry. It was completely embarrassing to Sweets that he had lost all control of his stable in more than one way. Now, even Sweets was getting high on the same drugs that he had used to make his girls dependent upon him. So now, the roles were reversed and he was completely dependent on them more than they were on him.

But the final straw that broke the camel's back had been the robbery attempt at Relax. It had effectively ruined him. His uncle had killed off two of the attempted jack-boys, but the last one had apparently gotten the best of him and killed him. And with a shitty fucking .38 Saturday Night Special, at that. What were the odds? he asked himself. It simply was infuriating to him. But it was breaking his heart at that, his Uncle Tree was like a father to him.

His mentor...Shit, his everything and then some. Not even to mention that Relax had been Sweets' home base, his office. Now where would he be able to set up shop at?

"Fuck dem niggas, Unc," Sweets said aloud, as he poured out some for his dead Uncle out of his double cup of lean and Mountain Dew. "I'ma find that last muthafucka and kill his ass myself one day ... "

Sweets had been hitting the lean and molly pretty hard lately. Not to mention the flaka and roxys he'd been experimenting with as well. Shit, he thought to himself, I'ma hit everything I can HAAM, or Hard as a muthafucka, till I can get Unc out my head.

But he could never get his uncle out of his head. He kept seeing the stretcher leaving Relax, an arm with a white gold rolex hanging down from under the white sheet covering his whole body. The same rolex with the diamond bezel that his father had given Tree as a gift when he had beat a murder case on the Westside of Chicago.

He was gone now though. They were both gone. Relax was gone too. FEDs had come, and their Gang Task Force had boarded up Relax, pending the investigation of the three separate gangs that had been involved in the three separate bodies dropped there, since they knew that Josue's brother-in-law was a big figure in the Haitian Sensations as well. There was no telling how long that would take, but a few of Tree's girls had been arrested for prostitution and it was only a matter of time before they told and implicated Sweets in the prostitution and human trafficking ring his Uncle Tree, as well as he, had been involved in.

He reached out to his Y-Lo homie. Chacho, who he had been told now resided in Cien Fuegos, Cuba, 90 miles away from the tip of South Florida, on the other side of the island. Y-Lo's are a Cuban gang out of Miami, mostly contained in the Allapatah, Wynwood, and Hialeah areas, and Chacho was one of their, at that time, ranking members who had fled to Cuba after another Y-Lo member, Pucho, had informed on him, turning state's evidence for time off on his state sentence. Chacho had Pucho killed finally and then he ran to their plug's hometown of Cien Fuegos, where the U.S. had no authority, nor even as much as an extradition treaty established with the communist country, making him out of the reach of the long arm of the American law. Safe.

Sweets knew that he would be accepted with open arms in Cuba, where he could start his stable off all over, and he knew he could be an even bigger success than he was in Palm Beach County. His American-born girls were all kinds of exotic, even to Americans, white; Puerto Rican; Haitian; and more, but with him being a crazy mix all himself, he could pull even more Cuban girls over there. But there is nothing more exotic to Cuban men than American girls. They hated them so much that they loved them. The line between love and hate being very thin, taken along with the fact that they were so rare in Cuba would be irresistible. They might tell their fellow compatriots that they would never speak to an American, but it is common knowledge that those are the main ones that are always sneaking off in the middle of the night to trick off with the exotic American girls. Yea, Sweets thought to himself, I'll do just fine over there. He thought it was a shame that none of his mother's side of his family still lived there in Cuba. They were all from Santiago, which wasn't that far from where he was in Cien Fuegos. But they all had migrated to South Florida now as well. Still, he would do just fine. Now, he would be grateful that his mother had raised him speaking Spanish and that he is fluent in it.

He had already told the girls, who were currently complaining, while in their room where they thought he couldn't hear them talking shit. All of a sudden, he heard a sharp scream and some commotion, as well as some crying going on. As he started walking over to their room, his blood started to boil over. As if he could help this shit? he said, talking to himself. Fuck it. He continued on back and was surprised when all of the girls were hugging on Sweet C in sympathy for some enigmatic feminine reason that he couldn't seem to understand. All heads turned towards him. All of them had hatred barely hidden in their eyes.

"What's the fucking problem wit ch'all bitches? Get ch'all shit packed up so we can get on! We got them peoples finna come at us at any minute-" he started.

"Sweets, Tasha say that it's Celiane daddy that be done got shot over to Relax. She said that Marquita and 'Lil Bit said-he was only trying to get Celiane back and-"

"Bitch!" snapped Sweets as he slapped the shit out of Brat, the tiny 4'11 Mexican girl who had kids from her sister's baby daddy, didn't raise any of her kids, and who was normally hated by most of the other girls. That was, until now. Even Scarface Nicky came to her aid down on the floor. Brat was one of Tree's pretty little dancers and still hadn't been broken yet, but Sweets now knew he had to break her, sooner rather than later, or she would turn the others against him.

"Hey, Sweets, take it easy, baby," said Nicky, ever the pleaser.

"Bitch, what you said?" he asked, kicking her in her ribs as she sat on the floor next to Brat, trying to comfort her. Sweets was shocked when her disposition changed suddenly and dramatically.

She screamed bloody murder as she jumped up like a crazy person, rushing towards him with her blade in her hand. As she started swinging her straight razor-something she had always kept on her ever since her run in with Celiane while they were all high on flaka tweaking out, her face having been severely cut by a box-cutter as a result. She swung right and left, Sweets ducking and weaving both wild swings with his quick athletic agility.

Finally, Sweets stepped back, preparing. During her next swing of the blade, she screamed again as she swung. Sweets blocked it with his left arm, turned into her, then grabbed her right wrist with his right, spinning her in front of him and placing her in a simple headlock, or at least meaning to.

What he had intended to be a simple headlock had become complicated by the fact that he had spun her with his empty left hand. He then, in one quick motion, put his right arm around her throat, getting more then he bargained for in doing so.

The problem was that her hand was still holding the straight razor and his arm had collected her hand, the razor, and her neck, all at once, crushing them all into the crook of his elbow.

Normally, this wouldn't have been a problem, but here, it was a huge problem and a fatal mistake on his behalf. One that ended up costing them dearly. The razor's edge connected with Scarface Nicky's neck, and ultimately her carotid artery, immediately severing it-as well as Nicky-from the blood to keep her brain functioning. Nicky would not be joining them in Cien Fuegos after all, or anywhere else, for that matter. Nicky's 18 year old life had been ended that fateful day. That quickly.

In all honesty, Sweets really didn't give a flying fuck. Nicky had been a drain on his resources now that she couldn't model, dance, or even give hand jobs at the jack shack. Although, he would miss what she could do with that tongue ring of hers, he couldn't care less about losing that dead weight, and it was a lot of weight that she had. She was more of a liability than an asset, so inside, he was happy. But he knows that he can't show his indifference though. Not in front of all of the other girls who expected him to actually care about them all, and he definitely knew that they were all watching him, trying to sense his reaction.

No matter what his true feelings are for Jolly, or Scarface Nicky, as she was known as affectionately within the house

154

recently, Sweets knew that he had to put on an Academy Award winning performance to stay in between 'daddy' and boss, so he cried and screamed. He basically put on everything he had for their benefit.

"Aww! Naw! Aww, baby girl! I ain't meant it! I'm sorry, baby, please don't die on daddy! It was only an accident ... Oh my God, what have I done ... ?" he said, trailing off and crying his best to show that he cared before he would have to use his pimp hand on the rest.

The girls were all crying. Sweets adapted his mournful look to fit his dual emotions that he would need to show them all: A strong pimp, yet still hurting and upset for losing someone that was so important to him as a man. But these girls must always be reminded that a pimp's mind is stronger than theirs, and that is why he needed to lead, and also why they needed to follow his lead without question.

Sweets wiped his dry eyes as if they were pouring tears, sniffled with his nose, and stood up, covered in Scarface Nicky's blood, like a vampire or some kind of demon. "What are y'all doing? Get your shit packed! Now! We leavin' in ten minutes to go to the boat dock and get our shit loaded up. Remember what I said, 'only what you can carry yourself'," he said simply.

"What about Jolly, daddy?" asked Nayla, who had become almost a little sister to Scarface Nicky in their last few months together in Thug Mansion.

155

"There's nothing we can do for her anymore, Naynay. C'mon, baby girl, she in Pimp's Heaven now, hoeing for Michael and Gabriel. We gotta let her go now." He then bent down reverently, continuing to put on his act, as if nominated for an Oscar Award, and he closed her eyes gently with his fingertips.

"Now, let's go! We gotta go before them peoples come for us ... come on, girls," he said quietly, still acting affected by her loss. He thanked Jesus that the girls finally started moving. He was really sad because of the necessity of leaving his beautiful car, Bella behind, more than he was going to miss Nicky.

§§§§

Celiane watched as Sweets wiped the non-existent tears from his eyes. All the others might be fooled by his acting capabilities, but not Celiane. She could see straight through his facade as if he were transparent. He didn't give a fuck about her friend, Nicky. She knew now, that she and the other girls were just tools to him. Assets. Things that could easily be manipulated and disposed of after he had no more use for them. Of course she knew that it had been an accident. Like hitting a stray cat or dog with your car. Except that she knew Sweets wouldn't pull over or stop if he actually hit one. He was really an evil man underneath his facade, his mask. She knows that his evil runs deep into his soul, and she could see it now that he is unmasked.

Celiane had been in the 'love bubble' for the last seven months-

blind even-but she no longer has the blinders on. She is now wide awake. She now knows how she had been tricked. Played, yet again. She wasn't sure she would have been able to face it again. The last time, Polo, the damn school bus that had failed to take her life, it had all been too much for her.

This time though, she knew that she could face it. She wouldn't even attempt to kill herself. She would fight. No, this time she would survive. She would become a survivor, and she would persevere. She would push through and come out stronger, she wouldn't have been able to do so otherwise, but knowing what her father had just been through-being shot, arrested, and charged-to what he had sacrificed: His own freedom, and two of his friends' lives, she knew that she couldn't let it all have been in vain. She wouldn't give in or quit.

As Celiane was trying to think of a way to get away from Sweets, their Uber minivan had just pulled up to the Yacht Club, where Sweets' Y-Lo homie was meeting them in Hollywood, which is south Broward County, off of the inter-coastal waterway. When they were pulling up, she saw a '35 cabin cruiser with a shiny black finish on its hull, and chrome trim and accessories. She saw two bulky Spanish-most likely Cuban-guys coming toward the van with the intention of helping them get their things loaded onto the boat.

Celiane's heart sank. There was no way for her to escape now. What could she possibly do? she asked herself in a panic. She looked around frantically until she spotted a public bathroom and a sign indicating there were showers within for the people who lived on their boats tied to the moorings or docked there. She slipped away towards the safety contained within. She knew it would have to have a window facing the opposite direction where she would be concealed from the boat and from the Uber minivan's line of sight. She would then crawl out of that window, keeping the bathroom building behind her, so they wouldn't see her getting away, escaping a hell she hadn't even known had existed until she met the real Sweets in Thug Mansion. Once she got down the street, the Tri-Rail train station wasn't far and she knew from experience that she could slide into a bathroom on the train until it made it to her Lake Worth stop at the Lake Worth High School train station.

Celiane was about to go into the bathroom, thinking about her whole escape plan in her head, step by step, she couldn't wait to see her baby brothers and to be able to tell her mother and father how sorry she was and how much she loved them and-

"Going somewhere?" an ominous voice asked her, while interrupting her thoughts and plan, as a heavy hand gripped her shoulder and her whole body was spun around in one quick motion.

"To ... Ah-to the bathroom," she responded, to one of the heavily tattooed and muscled Cubans, already shaking his head with disappointment, and her knowing that it was all over. She would never escape Sweets, or this personal hell that was now, her life.

"The bathroom is on boat. C'mon birdie, you can't fly away

easy ... "

And with that, she was being re-caged. Her karma, or fate, she supposed.

Chapter Fifteen

"Okay! Okay! Man, just please keep me out of it! It's Lexi Marley, that's who I've been giving the files to! She's using the names and social security numbers of deported aliens to rent houses and pay for insurance policies, and a lot of other shit too ... Please man! Just let me go!" A voice cries in anguish while obviously scared enough to most definitely be telling the truth.

"You're saying that was Lexi GAMBINI!? From the *Gambini* family?" asked Wicks' incredulous voice on the recording playing on his new iPhone 15 Pro, before he hit the pause icon on the touchscreen and a silence took over the room at the Red Roof Inn, not far from the Youth Center on 45th Street, where Wicks had asked Lexi Marley to meet him to discuss a 'mutually beneficial' proposal.

The silence deepened and overtook them all, Wicks knowing how powerful this woman is, forefront on his mind. Still, he said nothing, comfortable enough in the silence and allowing her to open the dialogue. Finally, after a long pause, she did.

"I will give it to you. It has been a very long time since I've met someone with balls like yours-fucking elephant balls to be precise-Mr ... Pierre, is it?" she asked, lazily, as if she hadn't already done a full background check before meeting with him, or as if she wasn't really a coiled rattlesnake, waiting for the right moment to strike. Wicks knows her type from his 13 years in a Federal Maximum Security US Penitentiary, so he is not impressed. Still, he is always going to be cautious, never going to underestimate an opponent.

160

"I've got no intention of keeping this-matter of fact-I'll delete it now, before we get to why I've come to you here." He deleted the recording as she looked on.

"Now I'm really confused. Isn't the point of having a 'one up' on me, to negotiate from a position of strength? That's chapter six in Sun Tzu's "*The Art of War*", right?" she asked, flipping her beautiful mahogany curls, her pretty face scrunched up in confusion. Wicks was taking in her figure, not in lust, but in simple curiosity. She is really quite beautiful at almost 6 foot in heels, and her double D-cups were barely able to stay contained in her red Prada business suit jacket. But he reminds himself that she must never be underestimated because of her book cover, becoming the first "Made" woman in the Mafia's history-she has put in a lot of work and is suspected to be behind even more murders than her own father, Antonio Giavanni Gambini, the Mob boss of South Florida.

"Like I said before ... 'mutually beneficial', so I'm gon' be the first one to play nice. By the way, I didn't in any way seek you out, Lexi. I ran across this information on a piece of business for my employer, Mr. Kline, and I see no reason for anyone to know anything about you. I do however, want those original files back, so at least my employer knows that I'm doing my job. You do understand, don't you? " asked Wicks nonchalantly, still watching closely for her reaction.

"And then, what? You expect me to believe that you're not intending to blackmail us with other copies of those rats dropping mixtapes-even though they brought their little situations on themselves?" she asked cynically, not yet knowing Wicks, only his reputation.

"Listen, I work at the Youth Center down the street there, so any favor I would ever ask of you would never run outside of helping the Youth Center, or any of the kids, really. I give you my word on that," he retorted.

Lexi's face almost imperceptibly softened for a split second and only a little bit. "Are you fucking serious?" she feigned cynicism.

One look at Wicks' hardened, tattooed face and she hesitated. "You know, I've talked to Antoine, and the old man in Matamoros," she said, referring to Antione Jean, head of the Haitian Sensations drug cartel, and 'El Senor' of the Gulf Cartel in Matamoros, Tamualipas, Mexico. "Both of them assured me that you were a worthwhile friend to have. My connections in the Palm Beach County Sheriff's Office have heard of you but have no interest in you, which tells me that you are either lucky, careful, or incredibly smart. Or even more highly unlikely, maybe all three. Either way, from all I've heard about you, it seems I could do a lot worse in the friend department. I also look into your eyes and think you are a man of your word. But, I must ask you this: If I do return those files to you, and I'm not saying that I have them, what makes you so certain that your employer will stand by our little agreement and not go to the police?"

A good question, thought Wicks, and in the right direction ... she is at least considering his proposal.

"Because I will take full responsibility and make sure he lets sleeping dogs lie. I believe to him, it was more about cleaning his car," Wicks said enigmatically, indicating his having to further elaborate.

"Ahh, the Federal Prison lingo-'a car', group or gang ... " she replied, to Wicks' astonishment at not having to explain his meaning. "Yes, most of the Gambini Family have done time in the Maximum Penitentiaries of the Federal system, so I am well-versed in lingos. He just wanted to purge his own law office of his definition of the rats or moles, no?"

"Exactly," said Wicks, smiling his mouth full of 20 gold slugs, permanently implanted in his mouth, as he is obviously impressed with her astuteness, as well as her quick wit. Before Wicks could begin to elaborate, his iPhone rang and he checked the display, though already knowing who it is. "Well, I guess we'll see what happens now," he said before answering the call.

"Mr. Kline, how are you, sir?" he asked, before listening for a while. "Okay, well I think I might have found the boxes of files." He then looked at Lexi. "I've tracked Boatman and Green's movements and it looks like they've fled the area, but I'm heading out to a storage unit I've traced them to, so, if the files are there, should I leave it there? Or should I pursue them to South America, where I think he-okay, sir. No problem ... of course, you're welcome. Okay ... I'll call as soon as I'm back. Bye."

Lexi smiled, clearly impressed with his professional handling and manipulation of the situation.

"So ... he don't care 'bout nothing else. You've got my word, give me the files and it's a done dada. Then we both got someone we can call when we need a favor, ya feel me?" said Wicks seriously, hoping it could be this easy.

Lexi smiled again. A genuine smile this time. Not the coiled snake, man-eating smile she was known for having before she killed her victims. A real and satisfied smile. "I like you, Wicks. That's so weird. I never like anybody, but I like you ... " She looked at him again, smiled once more, and added, "I'll be in touch ... " She walked out.

§§§§

Later that day, after two of Lexi's goons had delivered the boxes of case files to a storage unit and texted the location to Wicks from a burner, ever so cautious, he went and collected them, using Mr. Kline's big red 4X4 truck to bring them back to the law office and closed the case. This was the best result Wicks could've hoped for. It might not have been the result Mr. Kline had wanted, since Boatman and Green had gotten away, but any other result might have put Mr. Kline's life in jeopardy, dealing with Lexi Marley and the Gambini Family, so it was the best that he could do or hope for under the circumstances.

Now Wicks, or better yet, Jean Pierre, was the official private investigator for the Law Offices of C.F. Kline. Since Celiane's case was temporarily stalled, he needed to get some work done on his work load of other cases, now that he had secured the actual job. Alex Boatman had left him with two divorce cases-claiming infidelity-that he needed to gather evidence on, specifically some evidence of the cheating spouse. He also has a workers compensation case, where they were defending an accusation of fraud by the employer's workers comp insurance company, and then on top of that, he has the whole criminal defense of Celiane's father to investigate and his favor for Michel, having been hired to track down and bring Celiane home. The favor part was that 'hopefully' the pimp, Sweets, would be a collateral damage in the fight to rescue Celiane, or at least that was Michel's wish, a wish that Wicks had no problem granting him.

Wicks didn't care, one way or another. If he didn't kill this pimp, Michel's people in the Haitian Sensations cartel would definitely be happy to end his life for him. One way or another, Sweets was a dead man walking, and it wasn't going to be an opened casket funeral either. More likely a cremation.

Wicks' phone rang. He checked the display. Shelby. He smiled unintentionally. The mysteries of the way love works.

"Hey, baby, " Wicks answered her call immediately on his bluetooth. He listened to her speak for a few minutes, wrote down an address in Manalapan and mumbled his goodbye before heading downstairs to the parking garage, and his 1978 Buick Riviera in the condo's secure garage of their shared condo at the Moorings of Lantana.

Wicks pulled up to a Manalapan mansion only five minutes later, Manalapan only on the other side of the Inter-coastal Waterway from the Lantana condominium building. After ringing the fancy doorbell, the big gothic door opened. A slim, blonde, obvious model in a robe was revealed. "Wow, I hope you're the boy in this girl-boy-girl scene we're shooting today." Wicks didn't even crack a smile. He is a very focused person. Not easily distracted.

"Where's Jordan Jewels?" he asked seriously.

"He's in the back, are you going to ... " she started to ask him, but he had already moved in past her, heading to the back pool area of the mansion. As he passed through the sliding glass doors and out onto the screened-in pool area, he could see a sex scene being filmed, two guys and a girl. They were both trying their very best to fill every orifice of the poor girl, as if she were a Chinese finger trap, only not for fingers. Wicks ignores it all and is still focused though.

Wicks quickly picked out who had to be Jordan Jewels and made his way over to him, bumping into standbys and not caring. "Jordan?" Wicks asked the tall blonde man just starting to lower his Nikon professional camera. The camera has a foot long lens, as if he were trying to compensate for other areas of the anatomy that he might be found to be lacking in.

"Ye-" Jordan didn't get a chance to even finish an answer, before Wicks punched him in the nose with a left hook, not breaking it, but definitely turning it into a blood faucet, dripping blood all over his Polo shirt.

"Where is Celiane?" Wicks calmly asked him and then backhanded him before he could even formulate an answer.

"Wha-huh? You just fucking hit m-" Again, Wicks smacked the very shit out of him.

"She was 16 years old and you were taking naked pictures of her, so I know you know where they at! Tell me now!" Wicks punched him in his gut. There were several gasps and even some of the many people on the patio started making their way to leave after hearing about the photographer having been photographing an underage girl.

"Man, I-" started Jordan, before Wicks lifted his fists threateningly and at the ready.

"Fucking lie to me! Please fucking lie, so I can beat you like your ass deserve to be beat for taking advantage of a sweet and inexperienced teenage girl, I dare you to even fucking think a damn lie! I dare you!" Wicks shouted, as nobody even attempted to intervene for Jordan against this tattoo faced-gold mouth-lunatic.

Smacking him again had the desired effects, like a bully trying to get Jordan to give up his lunch money, he finally caved, before the Wedgie happened.

"Okay! Okay! Jezz, man ease up, I-" he started, trying to stall for time until Wicks went into his shit, punching him in the jaw, this time doing permanent damage and dislocating it. "Fuck! BLACK DIAMOND BLACK DIAMOND BLACK DIAMOND MAN! Damn! I did a couple photoshoots at Thug Mansion! It's Sweets' house in the Black Diamond neighborhood, out in Wellington. Jezz, man, I-"

"Gim'me your phone," interrupted Wicks, calmly waiting for the cameraman to place the phone in his hand. When he did, Wicks typed his own number in it and called his phone to get this asshole's number. He handed the phone back to the sniveling coward of a pervert, as he is sitting there choking and bleeding all over the pool deck like a caught fish out of water-dying and looking pathetic.

Wicks felt nothing for him. Empathy isn't something Wicks has an abundance of, and he wouldn't use the little bit he had on a scumbag like Jordan. Anyone who would abuse a bright future, taking it away from a teenager, would get no sympathy from him.

"I am driving straight from here to Wellington. To Black Diamond. I have a very fast 403 Olds under the hood. If you haven't texted me the street address by the time I get there, I will come back here .. You don't want me to come back here, now do you?" Wicks looked around at the few remaining witnesses and elaborated on his intention. "None of you do ... and oh, if you try to run, I'll find you. See, that's what I do. That's who I am. Nice to meet you all. And you-" He jumped at Jordan, who understandably flinched. "No more underage shit. If I find out, I come back and I kill each and every one of you motherfuckers involved, understood?" Wicks asked, finally walking away after seeing all of the affirmative head nods, as if they were a bunch of fucking bobblehead dummies, too petrified to utter a single word. Wicks doesn't care though. Wicks is a man of focus, and as long as his point has been taken and he has got Celiane's location, he would move on to his next step. His next mission. Being a man of focus allowed him to easily concentrate on what he had right in front of him without distractions, and right now, that was the need to get Celiane away from the life she had obviously been tricked into, and home to her family. Where she belongs.

He set out for Wellington. Black Diamond, located on 441 and Forest Hill Blvd. "Thug Mansion"? Wicks laughed to himself. What a douche bag this Sweets must be. Who names their house? What is it-like the Double D Ranch out in the old West? Would they meet at the OK Corral? What a douche, thought Jean, just now coming forward, after Wicks had finished his job. It is normal for him to relinquish the drivers seat back to his calm, less intense alter ego. But he wouldn't be far. He never goes too far, as he is often needed infrequently and unexpectedly. Thug Mansion, thinks Jean laughing. Unbelievable.

Chapter Sixteen

It had taken almost a month, but after Detective Shelby Nash had done an illegal search on her I.A.D computer data base and come up empty on Celiane or Sweets, she decided to go catfishing with her fake social media profile on Instagram. All of her pictures were the worst ones that she could find of Jayda Cheaves, the rapper Lil Baby's ex-girl. She picked out all dark or out of focused pictures, so nobody could say for sure who it was, yet still unmistakably identify the pictures as an amazingly stunning girl, someone they would definitely want to talk to.

She used this profile to secure leads and to entrap corrupt cops, but it also worked for her purposes today, finding Celiane and Sweets. She found them both on Insta and Onlyfans and then finally she was able to trace some of Celiane's first photos taken by a photographer working for Zivity.com, a guy named Jordan Jewels.

After giving Wicks the heads up and allowing him to chase down that Jordan Jewels lead, she did some more of her own catfishing, talking to several girls who had worked at Relax and got even more information on Tree, who turns out to be Sweets' uncle. Unfortunately, she also came across some Insta and Facebook chatter that places Sweets and his whole stable in Cuba, as of last night.

Shit, she thinks to herself, as she is patrolling social media sites, this information was definitely not good. But it also seemed like accurate and reliable intel as well. Definitely not good at all for the home team though. Cuba is a communist country, certainly the same direction that America was headed in under Biden's socialist agenda, thought Shelby. But, Cuba has no extradition treaty-hell, Americans weren't even supposed to be allowed to visit over there without extreme vetting and permission from everyone all the way up to the Beard himself, or whoever the new Beard is now. Impossible that some lowlife con-man pimp had already made it over there while we are hot on his trail, thought Shelby incredulously.

She decided to go ahead and do more research on this Sugarbaby.com profile she had run across. Sugarbaby.com is a social media-type site where girls-or boys-go to pick up a sugar daddy-or sugar mamma-to take care of them financially and buy them extravagant gifts. The sugar daddies and sugar mammas go there to find sugar babies they can sponsor. She located an address where gifts can be sent to Celiane, but unfortunately, the address was on 10th Avenue North, west of Lake Worth City. Relax, the jack shack where Sweets had been pimping out of, until Celiane's father had attacked and turned it into a crime scene, never to reopen again.

Shelby's phone vibrated, showing Jean's picture, identifying the caller.

"Hey bae, I was just about to-" Shelby started, answering his call, before Wicks had interrupted, silencing her with the seriousness of the situation in his rapid-fire rendition of his side of the events.

She listened for a few minutes as she gathered her things from office, leaving in a haste, trying to understand what was really going on. "Well, did you touch anything?" She again listened to him explain his predicament, trying to collect intel and plan, simultaneously.

"Okay, listen to me, did anyone see you or your car? No? Are you sure? You do realize that your car stands out and-" She listened again. "Okay, get out of there and text me the address and I'll handle it from there ... " She was on her way to the Black Diamond neighborhood. They had located Sweets' honeycomb hideout. Thug Mansion, he had said. Unfortunately, that's not all he had found there. She called the scene in anonymously.

§§§§

An hour later, Shelby was on the scene, explaining to a young, wet-behind-the-ears rotation detective about her, or more specifically, IAD's interest in a non-police involved death. There should be, quite literally, no reason for her to be there, and they both knew it. She definitely tried her hand at playing it off though.

"It's in loose relation to Detective Rodriguez, who I arrested a few months ago in a human trafficking ring. I'm sorry, but anything more than that is IAD classified. So, what do we have here? Who's the vic?"

"Vic's name was Nicole Foster," started the green detective, apparently accepting and not calling her on her "IAD classified" bluff, to her relief.

"Cause of death and TOD?" she followed up.

"Somebody slit her throat pretty good, but the blade was in her right hand, so we will let the M.E. determine the sequence of events. He's already given the TOD to be between nine and ten last night and-"

"He can place the time of death so close?" she asked.

"Well, the heat was off and last night got a little bit chilly being January, and according to the first arriving unit, the doors were left open, as if they left in a hurry-"

"They?"

"Well, let me show you..." he said, leading the way into a long hallway with several opened bedroom doors, hangers laying haphazardly everywhere.

Shelby touched nothing and was wearing crime scene 'footies' which fit over the wearer's shoes, as to not cross-contaminate the scene of the crime. She peeked in the first three rooms, assuming the rest were in the same condition. There were empty hangers, half empty bottles of shampoo and conditioner, random papers and empty bottles with their prescription labels removed, devoid of names or medication types, raising her curiosity. She ignored all of the scattered boxes of condoms.

"Bag and tag all of those pill bottles," Shelby instructed, pointing.

"Ma'am?"

"I want all of those bottles analyzed. The labels were removed for a good reason and I want to know what was in them. That might help us find out who they belonged to."

"And we can find out all of that just by sampling the bottles' residue?" he asked in astonishment, not yet familiar enough with the forensic techniques to be confident.

"Well, maybe not all of that, but you'd be surprised what kind of shit the labs can come up with. Make sure when forensics process the house for prints, that they also process that pretty candy apple car that says 'Bella' on the license plate as well ... "

"Yes, ma'am," the humbled detective answered.

Shelby was now sure that Sweets had fled the coop and now, she would have access to this scene to see if she could gather any more information on where they had went. Shelby started canvassing the surrounding, neighbors' houses, looking for a Ring doorbell camera, not only to catch their getaway vehicle and track that, but also to make doubly sure that Wicks' car didn't appear on the Ring footage, even though he did say he had parked down the street. She always did her due diligence.

Chapter Seventeen

Celiane was overwhelmed with misery in her new life and new environment. She and all of the girls-from Sweets' and Tree's stables combined-were being kept in jail cell-type rooms, as if they were being punished like common criminals. The worst part was the never-ending line of men that had been coming into her cell, having their way with her, and then leaving, only to make room for the next pig to come in and abuse her. She couldn't believe that this was now her life, her future. She's hurt. Not only the soreness in between her legs and her rectum, but mostly, the worst pain was in her heart. She is completely and utterly heartbroken.

This is not how things were supposed to be when she had turned sweet 16. She was in love. Sweets had doted on her, made her queen of Thug Mansion, and treated her like his most valuable gift. Like his wife, his partner. They had made plans. Even up until the shooting had happened at Relax, she was yet to even process all of the information she now held, about how her dad and a couple of his friends had tried to go to Relax to rescue her. To get her back. Now his friends were both dead and her dad was shot and awaiting trial for his life for three PBLs and it was all her fault. She had caused all of it herself.

Things had changed months ago. At first, when she had first started modeling, she had been doing these cute, sweet little Zivity.com shoots. It was actually fun for her. She began to enjoy

175

it. Then the drugs had taken a toll on Sweets. And then on her as well. Things quickly went downhill, spiraling further down and into a deep, dark hole with no way out. First came the soft core, webcam type of masturbatory pornography and Onlyfans shows of very graphic displays to subscribing fans interacting with her, which wasn't all that bad. But shortly thereafter, it had escalated to on camera sex with older men as partners-kind of porn. Multiple partners at that. It quickly progressed from there to greater, or actually, lower heights that she didn't even want to contemplate anymore than she had to. Couldn't even think of. She wanted it to be over with already, and although she promised for her father's sake that she wouldn't again try to kill herself, she wasn't sure how much more she could take of this. This was all worse than hell could be.

Celiane had her eyes closed, her thoughts on other things, fantasies of an escape that she could only dream of, as the black-skinned Cuban on top of her finally stopped pumping in and out of her swollen and sore vagina, finally having climaxed inside of her. He quickly got up off of her, put on his clothes, and without a word or even looking back, he left.

She let out a small sob. She couldn't understand why this was even happening, but she knew it wasn't getting any better. Only getting worse. Then immediately, it did. A Cuban policeman came in and pulled his pants down, pointing to his small, flaccid penis hanging in a curtain of pubic hair, almost hiding, as if suddenly shy or ashamed.

176

Celiane turned away, a single tear drop falling down her still quite beautiful face. She looked up at him, praying for sympathy but finding none. His face was expectant. She didn't want to. But she knew that she had to. She knew they would make her.

He suddenly shouted something in Spanish that she couldn't understand. Then everything in her world went black and she could hear a ringing in her ears. Had he just ... hit her? she asked herself incredulously, while going into a sudden panic. This policeman? Had hit her? She couldn't deal with it, so she just closed her eyes and went back into her own thoughts, her fantasies of an escape that might never come.

Of course, even being in her thoughts with her eyes closed, she still felt her body being flipped over, heard him yelling, and the following grunts, after he had forcefully penetrated her anus, effectively sodomizing her for her non-compliance with his instructions in a language that she couldn't understand. The pain was too much for her, she began to move her hands to feel about, but all she felt was his belt and trousers on the floor next to her. His gun.

She started to wonder why things had gone so bad for her as soon as the boat had landed. They had given out so many sexual favors to be driven in a military truck from *Fuerzas Armadas Revolucionaria*, or FAR, which is what passed as the Army for Cuba, to get to the other side of the island, to Cien Fuegos. There they had met up with Chacho and his girl Tiffany, who goes by the name Tip. Once Chacho and Tip had brought them into their

177

own stable, everything had changed. Tip is a super-violent woman with a short temper and an understanding level of absolutely zero. Tip had already beaten each of the girls at least twice for something even as small as a simple question. Assuming control of the girls and establishing her dominance was Celiane's only guess, but Tip worked all of them relentlessly, with only time for small naps here and there while the line of men waiting to get into Tip and Chacho's brothel of prison cells, stretched all the way around the corner. A never-ending line of men wanting to buy time with these girls.

The men were supposed to wear condoms during vaginal intercourse, in order to keep the assets from getting pregnant and in turn keeping the money machine moving, but half of them didn't care, and the other half just went for anal or fallacio instead. So, Celiane's ass was really hurting her by now, as there was no lubrication but her own blood and feces for anal penetration.

The more Celiane thought about it, the only scenario that made any sense at all to her about their predicament was that Tip had taken actual control of Sweets and his whole stable. No other explanation made any sense as to why she had seen Tip several times a day, but only saw Sweets twice in her whole time there.

Both of the times she had even seen Sweets had been the only two times she had been allowed to take a shower. Sweets had given her that luxury and then taken her into a stage prop-like teenage girl's bedroom, somewhere in the adjoining house, and given her a laptop with which she was to conduct her webcam sessions with customers off of her Onlyfans page, making separate money for Sweets that he had intimated to her that he needed so that he could "get us the fuck out of here." She couldn't be sure, but she felt like he was afraid of Tip and Chacho, and that he was hanging on by a thread just being here. She tried to ask for help on the webcam, but then the power went out, so she didn't know if the message even got through or not.

From Celiane's point of view, Tip was only bidding her time to kill Sweets and take them all for her own. Celiane was almost certain Tip suspected how much money those accounts were worth and wouldn't risk losing all of that income. Times were hard enough as it was in Cuba, as Celiane had overheard how they had been extorted into paying a corrupt Cuban MININT, or Ministerio De Interior, government official for them to just keep their Onlyfans and Insta accounts running and have unrestricted access to the internet, as the Cuban government has complete control over its constituents' internet access. Cuba did not want any of its citizens seeing Americanized internet propaganda and possibly getting any ideas as to how different life could be for them in the States, or what freedom was really like. So, Cuba's deep seated hatred of the United States only justified the need for the internet restrictions, as they all knew, without a shepherd, the sheep would soon thereafter be scattered.

That was only a temporary road block though. Soon, Tip and Chacho would figure out how to install some spywear on the laptop, allowing them to catch all of the account passwords and thus take over all of those accounts. At that time, she knew that they wouldn't need Sweets anymore, and that was what seriously scared her. She could tell that Chacho was just as scared of Tip as Sweets was. Tip is about 5'10 and 250 pounds solid and was known to have knocked out a few men when they got out of line. Celiane knew that when shit was hitting the fan, they didn't call one of those muscle bound idiots who couldn't think for themselves, they called the cold and calculating Tip. She is the brawn and the brains, surprisingly enough. There wasn't a man, woman or child in Cien Fuegos who hadn't heard of Tip and also feared her gangsta. They all really respected and feared her. They had seen and knew what she was capable of.

Even though she now sees through him, just the thought of losing Sweets and being left on this Godforsaken island with the likes of Tip immediately kicked Celiane's mind into overdrive. What could she do, though, besides follow the plan she was given? she asked herself. The corrupt Cuban policeman's grunts and corresponding pumps had started to speed up and turn frantic, becoming erratic, as his continued rape of Celiane was apparently turning him on more than consensual sex would have.

A policeman, she exclaimed to herself as her light bulb came on. His trousers, his belt ... his GUN! The long barreled old revolver she remembered seeing, when he had dropped his trousers and ordered her to perform fellacio on his nasty ass little penis. Now, where was it? She remembered feeling his belt when she had been trying to avoid her rapist's advances. She began to slowly feel around, trying not to attract the filthy rapist's attention. But as she felt the belt, she allowed her hand to follow along its length until she felt the stiff leather of the gun's holster. It is her ticket to escape. She can wait no longer.

As she unsnapped the button that had been securing the firearm in the holster and made a small fake moan to cover the noise, she started arching her back, as if she was actually enjoying being raped and sodomized. Her rapist only grunted and spent his seed inside of her worn and bloodied anus in response to her fake enthusiasm.

As he pulled himself out of her unceremoniously, she ignored the pain and turned over onto her aching backside. It seemed as slow as if she could see each grain of sand as they pass through a minute timer. When her rapist finally looked up momentarily and locked eyes with Celiane, his own eyes grew as big as saucers when his brain finally beheld and registered the scene before him and what it meant for him. For his future-or lack thereof.

Her confident eyes were locked with his terrified ones. He broke eye contact first, after what seemed to be an eternity. His eyes drifted slightly downwards and to her hand, and what was contained therein. It was the last thing he ever saw and Celiane was the last girl he ever was able to rape. His attempt at communication was overpowered by his fate. A quick and deadly fate.

"Que-" he started, but his question was never finished, as the loud pop from his own gun in Celiane's hand ends his question ... and his life, in one quick moment.

Chapter Eighteen

A few days had passed since their discovery of the grisly scene found in Thug Mansion, in which Nicole Foster's body had been found brutally murdered by her own pimp, Sweets. Fingerprint evidence now connected Sandino Armand to the murder in a show of overwhelming physical evidence that he had at least touched or handled the bloody murder weapon. Shelby knew for a fact that in South Florida, juries would convict on a hell of a lot less than that. Sweets was on a wanted list, and Celiane and his other girls were all wanted for questioning in relation to the murder as well.

Shelby had decided to run a little game on the lead homicide detective on Nicole Foster's murder case-maybe get an 'in' inside of the investigation. It was his first murder investigation, and Shelby could still remember her own first murder investigation: one which she had actually solved the vic's murder on her own and then realizing who the vic had been, she didn't arrest the killer. She instead fell in love with him and then began a real relationship with him, after he had killed another man, an even more deserving man, while saving her before she almost lost her life.

She knew just how green someone could be on their first solo murder case, and she planned on using that to her advantage. So, in order to expedite things, she spun him a hypothetical situation in which she was investigating a dirty cop who might or might not have been involved with the other dirty cop she had arrested on the human trafficking case. So, for this reason, she needed Detective Evans to keep her involvement in the investigation a secret, as well as keep her abreast of all that was going on. Of course she made sure Evans knew that she wasn't supposed to let anyone know what she was investigating, but well, she "just knew" that she could trust him and she knew that he wouldn't spill the beans or jeopardize her case in any way. She giggled to herself a little bit at how easy she made him her unwitting eyes and ears into the investigation of her target, Sweets.

At first, she was happy at waiting on any leads through Evans until Wicks had talked her into pressing on, by helping him with his own investigation on Celiane's socials and Onlyfans pages. This is where Wicks had needed to shell out a little bit of his bitcoin collection that he had confiscated on a previous mission.

Wicks had set up a couple of webcam sessions with Celiane while Shelby had tried to follow the receiver's IP address. All that was a bust when they found out that it was a Cuban MININT government IP address, meaning that there was no location available for purposes of Cuban national security.

Wicks chose to follow the only logical next step: to actually put on a fake show, as if he and Shelby were really interested in using Celiane's webcam session and masturbation show as a marital aid to help get their own sex life-and ultimately their marriage-back on track. Once they were live, they wanted to gage whether Celiane was being monitored and so they put on as if unsure and embarrassed. They played like they wanted to get to know her a little bit first, as they had never done anything like this before and were just so shy. They had agreed that if they keep shooting random comments and questions, as if they were trying to decide whether or not they wanted to follow through, as if they were sure enough who they said they were and were just flaky enough to balk if anything felt less than rainbows and sunshine, she might give up her location on her own. At that point they could coordinate a rescue mission for her.

Once they got into a comfortable flow of things, they asked if she was being monitored so that they wouldn't reveal their real names, but Celiane must have sensed something in their intentions or maybe it was just testing the waters out when she spoke.

"He's not in here with me right now. He comes and goes, but I'm alone right now since he's setting the other girls up on their webcams and stuff."

After her revelation, they quickly told her who they really worked for and how her uncle had recruited them and then they worked out a code where she would be able to warn them if someone were to come into the room, and then they began to work with her on a plan to go and rescue her after hinting to her what they really did for their occupations. She let them know that she was locked out of her laptop's functions and apps, so she had no way to communicate more than being able to click and accept sessions on Facetime that are linked to her Onlyfans and Instagram pages, and that most of the webcam customers were sent to Celiane's page by Sweets and his network of womanagers and his own client base, using her Facetime functions.

As Wicks would ask her questions, keeping his thuggish looking face on the screen, in case her captors walked in, Shelby was typing furiously on her laptop, Googling Cuba-and the Cien Fuegos part of Cuba in particular, comparing it to the depiction on the Google Earth app. Finally, they agreed on a time, date, and a general area to meet at, picked from satellite images on Google Earth, where they might be able to effectuate a successful extraction. They were all black, so being as though they knew nothing of Cuba, they felt they would stick out less in the *Nichardo* areas of the city. Basically, the hood. *Niche*, or *Nichardo*, means black, or black Cubans.

Wicks and Shelby both took turns explaining an outline of a plan if she was able to get out of the compound that they suspected she was holed up in based on her description and their birds-eye view they were looking at on Google Earth. Celiane, in turn committed their faces to memory, so she would recognize them immediately when they met up. They at least felt they had a solid plan worked out, or at least the outline for one. They both have high hopes that they will be able to pull this off, although Wicks knows that he will not only have to enlist the help of his nephew, Marine Sergeant EJ Morzella, but also that of his

186

nephew's best friend, Station Chief Tyrone Bass, who goes by Ty, along with his CIA connections and equipment, to be able to pull off such a brazen rescue like this one was sure to be. It would be impossible to do without their support.

Even without speaking, to EJ or Ty, Wicks and Shelby knew one thing for sure and two things for certain: One, both EJ and Ty would both not hesitate to participate in this mission, and two, this would ultimately be the hardest mission or situation that any of them have ever faced. And either solo or collectively, they had all faced a lot of tough situations in their hard lives, just nothing like this before. Celiane's life was hanging in the balance and none of them were going to be willing to let anymore harm befall her after all that she had already been through. They were going to go and get her, bring her home safely and give her back to her family. Nothing could stand in the way of that. Nobody would stop them.

§§§§

Their confidence almost immediately started to waiver, when right before final plans could be made on the mission to Cuba, Shelby-who was still in some shit over the whole Detective Rodriguez bust and three bodies that had been dropped that night was called in by her boss' boss, John Eddards, Director of Palm Beach County's branch of Internal Affairs Division.

Surprisingly, Detective Rodriguez had been allowed out on

bond while awaiting a trial that almost certainly wouldn't come and while pending the investigation because of his many ties to the community and the weakness of the evidence or the case against him. In other words, as far as the powers that be were concerned, Shelby had fucked up majorly. She had no warrants for the surveillance recordings that she set up on the docks where she had found out Rodriguez was crooked because she hadn't planned on using anything that night in a court of law. That was her mistake. He had never been on anyone's radar. The powers that be didn't want to accept what Shelby had brought in, they also wanted to be made privy to all Shelby's investigative history on him to see what they missed.

At that point, Shelby had faltered. The thing was, she couldn't produce any of an investigative history because there hadn't ever been one. Just like the powers that be, Shelby had looked into Rodriguez, yet had never found any indication that he had been corrupt. So, she had never suspected him. He was extremely smart to have gotten away with it for so long.

Now, Rodriguez's lawyer, Roberto Norvelli, a corrupt Mob criminal defense attorney, was calling for open season on Shelby's badge, as well as filing motions to suppress evidence based on "fruits of the poisonous tree" because she had never applied for surveillance warrants or even sworn an affidavit to obtain one for Rodriquez.

"So, where the fuck is all this coming from, Boss-" started Shelby.

"Don't fucking call me 'boss', Nash! I'm just as upset about this bullshit as you are. And yea! That's another fuckin' thing," said Eddards. "Who in the fucking holy hell is Nicole Foster? And how is this connected to the Rodriguez shit?"

"Rat bastard-" started Shelby.

"Excuse me?" shouted Eddards, interrupting her sotto voce condemnation of the green Detective Evans. Apparently, he hadn't been as green as she had hoped. Even more so, it was obvious that he had called in favors and checked up on her for being on his crime scene. Great, she thought to herself, now how the fuck do I explain away this mess of an alleged connection? A connection, that in all actuality, didn't even exist, since she had been throwing out the Rodriguez investigation in a panic, trying to have an excuse ready for IAD to have an interest in a non-police action crime scene. What a fucking clusterfuck she had gotten herself into.

Eddards, being at a loss for words and getting no explanation from Shelby, had really been left with no choice but to place her on administrative leave, at least, until they could get a handle on what the hell was really going on and what was "connected" to what...

Shelby wasn't concerned in the least about facing the board on this shit with Rodriguez. To her, it didn't matter how she found out that he was dirty. The cat was out of the bag, the important factor-what the recordings proved-was that he was in fact dirty.

He was connected to Lemonhead and Haitian Sensations. It would have come out eventually, and even if they suppress the tapes against him, Shelby knew he was no good, and she wouldn't give up until she had his ass in prison or with a bullet sitting securely inside of his brain, sending him to hell, where his corrupt ass belonged. But that would all come later.

All that Shelby could think about or concentrate on now, was the mission at hand. They all knew it wouldn't be easy. But Cuba? This would be like a whole different world to them. There are certain things that Shelby could relate-or at least-adapt to, but going to a communist country-no-sneaking into a communist country, where Americans are equated with Satan himself? This would not go easy. She knew it, but she was still going to be up for it.

She would back Wicks and Jean at anything, but to help little Celiane? She would break her back to help a 16 year-old girl from the monstrous reality of being pimped in a third world country. Everything Shelby does, went along with her overall goal of leaving the world a better place than when she got into it. That was her goal-ambition-and motivation, all wrapped into one. This mattered. She is finally ready to go and save Celiane. Celiane's life matters to Shelby. So, there would be no stopping her. Of that, she is certain.

190

Chapter Nineteen

Celiane's whole inner being froze in time immediately after the shot was fired. Her ears were ringing again, but this time, it wasn't from being hit. She had finally stood up and defended herself. She had made a move. She is no longer a victim. The ringing was actually from the loudness of the echoing gunshot inside such a small place where acoustics were brain numbing. She suddenly felt her body's excruciating pain, all in her legs and ass, but this time, it wasn't from being raped over and over again in a repetitive personal hell. It was because she hadn't realized until right now, that she was sprinting at full speed. Her soreness was now almost completely forgotten as she ran all the way down the long hall, waving the gun she had failed to let go of after shooting the corrupt pig of a Cuban police officer.

She didn't even yield when she came to the end of the hall as she had reached the exit door bouncer-looking guy. No, she just waved the gun some more as she approached him and he automatically stepped back and out of her way. He was there as muscle and he was dumb, but he is smart enough to know that he isn't bulletproof, and that they didn't pay him enough to be shot at.

When she finally made it out through the exit door, where the tricks would normally leave after their happy ending had been fulfilled, she was now inside of a walled-in courtyard. A few men were milling about, smoking and talking, but it didn't take more than a second for her to identify an opened black metal gate, leading out to the street that is bustling and busy with night-time activity and traffic.

She ran straight through the gate, her legs like pistons, pumping as they never had before because she was for the first time, literally running for her life. She had been running, so fast that she literally couldn't turn. Once she passed the exit gate, she ran right out into the street, almost immediately rolling her body over the hood of a 1950's Chevrolet taxi whose driver reacted by slamming on his brakes and banging his fist on a broken steering wheel that had a horn that hadn't worked in decades, as he was angrily cursing her out in his unknown native language.

She continued running, gun still clutched in her hand. She continued on, despite her shortness of breath and the excruciating pain that her body was being exposed to by being pushed to its limits, after weeks of sexual trauma, as well as physical and mental abuse, in addition to the exhaustion she had been suffering. But she couldn't slow down, she wouldn't stop. She had to get far enough away where they couldn't find her. She is black-skinned, but in Cuba it is easy for her to blend as *chardos*, or black-skinned Cubans, who are even more common than green-eyed white Cubans. She just needed to find her area. A black *barrio*. She was told by Wicks and Shelby that black Cubans had their own areas over here, where they would feel comfortable amongst each other, so Celiane knew, as they had discussed, she

192

just had to find her area and get in where she fits in, then try to find her rendezvous point.

Celiane began looking all around her, looking for the signs she had been told were around her area in Cien Fuegos as she continued running. She could see a small building with loud music coming out of it. A pool hall. She had been told about it. She was on the right track. Her benefactors had told her where to go and when to do it. She just didn't wait. She couldn't wait one more minute. She had seen an opportunity and she had seized it. *Carpe diem*, as the Latin phrase for 'seize the day' that she had learned in her creative writing class, about a million years ago had said. Now, she felt stupid for not taking Spanish class. She had taken French for an easy A, being that she already was fluent in Creole, another dialect of French, as a first language.

She had indeed 'seized the day' fully today though, but now she was in deep trouble. Her benefactors weren't coming yet. She had went and jumped the gun days early. She had seen an opportunity and taken it. How could she have ignored it? What other chance would she ever have to put a gun in her hand and a bullet in her rapist's head? She had needed to make her move. She had to break free early. She couldn't take the abuse even another second. She would never allow herself to be abused again. If she could get out of this alive, that is.

She ran past a group of men outside of the pool hall that began whistling at her. She hadn't even realized that she was still completely naked until then. Naked, except for the gun in her hand, but that was an easy fix now.

"Give me your clothes!" she shouted at a small and very drunk black *chardo* walking along the sidewalk, as she had just passed out of sight of the front of the pool hall. He seemed not to understand as he pointed down to her very naked body, telling her that she is naked, it seemed. She almost began to cry still holding the gun but the man seemed to sense her need more than comprehend her words in the English language she was speaking and just shrugged off his long overcoat, handing it to her in a chivalrous way to cover her nakedness with. She said "thanks" and then started to run when he tapped her shoulder and pointed. Her eyes followed his short, crooked finger, pointing toward her previous captors from a hell she had been living for what seemed to be so long now.

Her eyes widened as she saw two Cuban police officers and a very big, and very pissed off looking Tip. All of them were checking parked cars and looking down alleyways. Looking for her. They began talking to the group of patrons outside of the pool hall who all immediately pointed in her direction. When Tip looked up through, Celiane had already run down the closest dirt alleyway, her bare feet sore from the rocks.

After lurking in alleyways and moving in the shadows, she realized she was starting to notice that she is tired and cold, beyond exhausted actually. She had been running for about an hour now and she was about an inch from crashing out. Tip and the policemen chasing her had knocked her off of the course that

194

she had been traveling on where her benefactors had described for her to follow and now she is completely lost without a map and still painfully walking barefoot. Under the man's jacket she was still completely naked, but after all the men-and objects-that had been forced inside of her, the nakedness is the least of her worries. She needed to find a safe place to hide, to wait it out. She kept on running though.

Coming up on another intersection, she decided that she could go no further as she was overcome by the pain and exhaustion, which sat her down on an overturned metal shopping cart missing all four of its wheels. The unstable cart crashed on its side, dumping her right along side of it onto the ground. Her fatigue had finally set in and taken over, Celiane sinking into a deep coma-like state, curling her used and abused body into a ball inside of the overcoat and giving into her overwhelming exhaustion.

Celiane slept. And slept. And slept some more.

She awoke to a dream. There is a little girl playing with her hair. Celiane reached up and felt small braids in her dirty and matted hair. The little girl smiled up at her, one front tooth prominent in her mouth, emphasizing her adorableness.

"Catalina! *Vete ahora!*" whispers a large black Cuban lady, causing the girl to issue one more parting smile, before running down the hall. The odd, yet first thing that Celiane notices-besides the fact that she isn't dreaming-was the bottoms of the little girl's feet were dirty and that the floor that she ran on was only packed dirt, not a floor. The small crib was more like a hut with no kind of foundation, which was a weird and novel thing to Celiane, her growing up in America and never leaving.

"Hello, girl. I am Marta. Catalina found you in the alley and we brought you here. I am very sorry. But now, you must go. .. "

Celiane was startled at the quick change in dispositions, seeing as though they had indeed rescued her. "But I have nowhere to go. Please, I have someone coming to get me, from Florida-"

"From America!?" she asked incredulously. "*Que no*! They will never make it onto the island! Cuban Coast Guard will get them! Look, I try to help you, but I can't risk my family. The Cien Fuegos police are all around, and with F.A.R. Also, they are all searching for you asking questions everywhere. They are communists! It is only so long before they are tipped off by *chevas* and come to search my house-"

"Don't they need warrants?" Celiane asked, interrupting her.

"No! *Loca*! This Cuba! They go where they want and search where they want . I sorry, but you must go, I will give you some bread and water, but you have to get moving. Every pair of eyes is an intelligence officer for the *Gobierno*, we cannot risk it. I am sorry, but we have to get moving. You must go."

Celiane quickly got to her unsteady feet, not wanting to bring any kind of harm to the wonderful little girl who had saved her or her mother, who had risked everything by indulging in her little girl's philanthropic whims.

But right then, as Celiane was trying on the ill-fitting clothes and shoes that had been laid out for her, she heard the latch on the flimsy wooden door break, as the door was suddenly kicked in and three black Cuban police officers rush in screaming things in Spanish that she doesn't understand. They all rush towards the crate she is sitting on and she automatically cowers in submission, knowing that she doesn't have even a slight bit of a chance at trying to resist them or run, as the shack only has one door in and out.

She was thrown on the ground while being simultaneously punched and kicked by these same men who were entrusted to uphold the law. Celiane knew she has no win here, but her last thought before being knocked back into unconsciousness is, that even jail or prison in Cuba has to be a lot better then what her fate would have been had she stayed in that little cell in the brothel she has been in. At least that much was over. Or so she thought, as her consciousness faded and her mind went back into Dreamland once again.

PART III

CUBA

exitus acta probat (Latin):
the outcome justifies the deed

Chapter Twenty

Once Wicks had gotten a hold of EJ, who in turn had contacted his friend and colleague-Ty, for his help, things started moving as fast as a speeding foreign in the far left lane on Interstate I-95. Ty had vetoed Wicks' plan of stealing or even renting a fishing boat and trying to blend in with other fishermen in the twilight hours that most fishing vessels tend to move about in. His reasoning ringing true to them all about the 12 miles surrounding the Island of Cuba and the vigilant Cuban Coast Guard, and how passionate and dedicated they are about not only keeping the Americans out, but also keeping their citizens in.

Ty had instead secured them transport on a military Apache helicopter as CIA spooks going to the U.S. Navel Base Station at the inlet of Guantanamo Bay in Southeast, Cuba, and they would then have to sneak out from the secured military base and go to Cien Fuegos from there to rendezvous with Celiane and escort her safely back home. Ty was risking a lot on this, while breaking every rule in the book, as this would not only break the international law and the Third Geneva Convention, but also the CIA's own rules for engagement in a communist country or dictatorship.

Wicks doesn't give a fuck about rules. He never has, and he never would. He's been breaking the rules since he was a kid and even though his priorities and reasons for breaking them have definitely evolved, his lack of respect for the law hasn't. He would get Celiane back even if he had to assassinate Castro himself-or whoever it is now that runs this mess of a communist government. He had given his word that he would bring her home to her mother and uncle, and that is exactly what he was going to do.

"You good, bae?" a feminine voice asked in his air-headphones, breaking into his thoughts like C-4 to an enemy structure as they ride to Cuba on the incredibly loud and fast helicopter.

"I'm good, I'm just hoping she is good ... " Jean answered Shelby soberly.

"I'm sure she's fine. We knew communication was going to be hard, don't worry, we're almost there ... " replied Shelby, addressing the facts that had them both worrying, on top of their already existing anxiety about the Detective Rodriguez investigation and Shelby's suspension from active duty.

It has been two days since they had last been in contact with Celiane on Facetime through her Onlyfans page for special webcam sessions, when the power had apparently went out twice in the middle of their planning, But for the last two days, it had been radio silence from Celiane ever since, hence the reason for their worrying. They had no idea what had been happening on her end.

Finally, the island came into view. It was only a 20 minute ride to Cuba, since Cuba is only 90 miles south of Florida's coast, where Cubans could even listen to some of Miami's radio stations, but with the stress everyone was feeling, the ride felt a whole lot longer. Everyone in flight knew what was at stake.

"It's beautiful, isn't it?" asked Shelby, almost in awe at the amazing view of the beautiful island.

"It won't be for long if they've hurt that girl .... " replied Wicks, replacing Jean and trailing off as the helicopter touched down on the U.S. Navel Base helo pad.

Wicks and Shelby, who were accompanied by EJ, Ty, and another Marine friend of theirs who only went by 'Serge', all jumped off of the helicopter and ran ducking under the still spinning blades to the man confidently striding towards them at the heliport, dressed in his battle combat uniform, or BCUs. He waved them over and indicated that they should follow him to a waiting military Humvee. Once they were all introduced, Wicks was able to deduce that this was one of the operatives that had served with EJ, Ty, and Serge over in Afghanistan, or Sandland, as they referred to it often. There was a high level of respect between them after such hard circumstances shared between them.

Martinez quickly distributed combat packs and AR-15 rifles to everyone who didn't already come prepared and began lacing them up as he led the way towards the path they would be taking. "Okay y'all boys, we going to have to sneak out of the compound and it's going to be tricky in a group, since the whole base is surrounded by armed perimeter guards as well as land mines. So we have to be precise. You step where I step, and once we get clear, ole' Serge here can use his childhood skills and steal us a vehicle. Listen, I'm all for my guys, but Ty, none of this shit better fall back on me, I'm just sayin'," said Martinez, a black New York Dominican who had been sneaking out of the compound to go trick with the beautiful and exotic looking Cuban girls in the nearby city for a long time.

"Don't worry, Marty. If worse comes to worst and the shit hits the fan, we've got Serge with us, we'll find an alternate route off the island," said Ty.

"Say less, " answered Martinez, as he led them along a path that looked like it ended at a razor wire fence. But looks are deceiving, as was the point.

The trail led to a fence, true enough, but up close, the jungle -like congestion of the trees had crowded the whole fence and at one place, a palm tree had grown leaning down, pushing up against the fence where it was quite obvious that they had been using it as a ladder to get up and over the fence. It was quite convenient actually. Beyond it, Wicks could clearly see the path in the brush leading, presumably to the nearest city of Guantanamo, where they could procure transportation to Cien Fuegos.

Wicks gave Shelby his shoulder to help her climb up the palm tree and then to climb over the fence, following Martinez and Serge. Wicks climbed up after, leaving EJ and Ty to bring up the rear. They all traversed the trail for about 15 minutes before reaching a small clearing with a few cows, and then a city not much farther beyond.

They could hear vague dance music and city sounds from the distance.

As they got closer, Serge took point and began looking for a vehicle. Due to their numbers, he was searching for a van or truck to be able to load them all into. Finally, he backed up in an all tan, mud splattered truck about 60 years old or more. American steel. A Chevy. Like a rock. How ironic, thought Wicks, as they all crawled into the back and Serge took off, starting the long drive to get to Cien Fuegos, and ultimately, to Celiane. Wicks is worried about her and the very slim chances of her being safe and unharmed at the top of his conscious. She has a very small chance of survival. He knows this. Especially in a communist country, where an out of place person can easily be spotted, usually quickly, reported to the regime for a reward.

"They better not have hurt that girl ... " said Wicks somberly.

"I'm sure she's fine. We'll get her baby, don't worry..." answered Shelby reassuringly, trying to put it out into the universe or speak it into existence, hoping for the best.

They were all hoping for the best though. They had to. There is no other choice, as failure is not an option. Celiane has nobody else in the world. Only them, and there was no back up to call or help to save the day, this was real life, not a movie.

Chapter Twenty - One

Tip, the real boss bitch of Cien Fuegos, paced her office in a fury. She was so livid to see Chacho and his lacky-punk-ass-homie, Sweets, just sitting there like they didn't know what to do. Lost puppies. As if sitting here in her office doing nothing was somehow a better idea than doing something. Doing anything. Anything but sitting right here in her face.

"So, not only did you two stupid muthafuckas-" she started.

"Now, Tip, hold on a minute ... " interrupted Sweets, as he looked to Chacho for support. He was surprised to see Chacho's head down, in submission. Eyes on the floor.

Tip waited patiently for the realization to sink in that neither he, nor Chacho for that matter, were running shit in Cien Fuegos, Tip does. "You interrupted me. You do that shit again, I'll put your brains all over that wall right there ... " she said, pointing towards a wall to his left that was stained brown, despite the obvious cleaning efforts that had been made to wipe past blood stains off it. Sweets was momentarily silenced.

"I fucking go over to Matanza for a fucking day, and you two idiots manage to not only lose one of our bitches, but-" Tip began again.

"Celiane is my-" started Sweets, already forgetting what Tip had said only seconds before. It was his last mistake ever. Tip reacted immediately.

Just as Sweets' mouth began to form the fourth word in the thought that had unintentionally bursted from his brain-lightning fast-Tip pulled her Kimber R-7 baby 9mm from her jacket pocket and put it up to Sweets' temple, quickly pulling the trigger and ending any further thoughts from him.

Her Kimber was loaded with 9mm hollow point ammunition, so upon entering his head, the hollow point expanded, taking the other side of his head completely off and painting her office wall with his blood, skull, and brain fragments.

"What the fuck! C'mon, Tip! That's my homie! What-" started Chacho.

"*That was your homie!* And stop being a 'lil bitch, too! Nigga, I'll put one in your ass-you keep tryin' me! I told your ass how that weak-ass nigga was just in da way! Now he ain't, and my-"

"But he's got all the passwords to the Onlyfans accounts!"

"Like I was trying to tell you ... my spyware on the laptops got the password, it's the same for all his accounts. 1973Bella. It's what he named his stupid car. What a flunky. Anyways, we got bigger problems, you not only lost that 'lil Haitian bitch, but you know we got Cuban police and F.A.R. up our ass, not to mention the MININT, now that she fuckin' shot Manera, so we are going to have to come out of pocket a lot for this fucking mess and it's going to make it hard to move around. I need you to talk to the captain and pay him whatever it takes to get them past this big fucking clusterfuck. Make an offer to compensate Sr. Manera's family-you already know who his father is-and get some of those young bitches on the Onlyfans accounts now! We need to make up for the loses right away. Now-"

"Why the fuck I gotta do all this shit?" Chacho asked, interrupting Tip's instructions, his question almost rhetorical.

"Because ... you fucking idiot, in this country, if they knew a woman was in charge of this whole operation, we'd have every cartel on the island gunning for us, the *Policia* and MININT wouldn't work for us and we'd be broke or dead. It's not my fault it's a sexist country, but yours is the face on the front, so do your fuckin' job and make yourself useful," said Tip.

Saying nothing, Chacho just suddenly left to go do as he was directed. Only a very select few knew that Tip ran shit. Everyone else pretty much figured it out by seeing her moves and watching how Chacho and other men deferred to her leadership. She liked to play the street tough gangsta-ette, but in reality, Tip is very smart. She is smarter than most in fact, but as a strategic move, she let her brutality be the outstanding attribute she allowed to be noticed about herself. If nothing else, Tip is indeed a deep strategist, a chess player, contemplative and careful in her movements. She only plays the role of the muscle, as underestimation of her intellect is a weapon all in itself and she used it to it's full potential.

Walking over to her closet, to the left of her desk, Tip

grabbed a big blue tarp and brought it over to Sweets like a present, unfolding it as she went, and spreading it out all the way. She pushed the body off the chair with her foot. Sweets landed on the tarp with a thud. She began to roll it up so she could carry his body out to her truck. Chacho had known better than to ask Tip if she needed his help, it was another of her pet peaves as an independent boss woman. She did her own dirty work, fought her own battles, and got blood under her own fingernails. Tip only needs a man for his face. As a puppet. Tip is self-sufficient, a real street gangsta, and that translates into the same thing, no matter where you are, or in what language you speak. She is a real boss bitch.

Tip heaved the weight of the body over her shoulder. She would be taking the boat out tonight. Take a ride south to a nice coral reef nearby that was populated by some very big and hungry sharks. It is shark feeding time, she thought to herself sarcastically with irony, I hope the sharks like "Sweets" ... she laughed to herself at her own dark humor, beginning to cheer up. Ding-Dong Sweets the pimp is dead. She laughed some more. Him being dead is the only silver lining out of this whole mess, so she had to enjoy that much.

Chapter Twenty - Two

As Celiane awoke in excruciating pain in a medical bay bed, she realized two things: First, that she was handcuffed to the side bars of the old and rusty medical bed. Second, she must have missed her meeting time with Wicks and Shelby by now, as those two days must have definitely passed already for sure.

She looked around and took in her surroundings. She was not connected to any machines-a good sign-yet she saw that she had an IV drip attached to her left arm. She tried to move and a sharp and unbearable pain originating from her ribs shot forth into her brain like a bullet. Celiane moaned and stilled herself immediately before she involuntarily screamed out. Looking down, she saw that her ribs were tightly wrapped up. She immediately flashed back to a vague memory of being kicked and stomped all about her face and ribs. She assumed that her ribs were broken as she could barely breathe. The pain was of a degree that she never had experienced before or even thought possible.

The last thing Celiane saw before passing out was a quite beautiful and exotic looking white Cuban woman with blue eyes and curly mohagany-redish like hair wearing blue scrubs coming toward her with a severe smile. Coming to help her. Save her.

Celiane slept restlessly. Nightmares of Cuban police and the F.A.R. chasing her haunted her throughout her slumber. It was repeated over and over until an angel would come forth, a blue-eyed nurse named Lizi, fighting for her safety.

Suddenly, a painful assault awoke her from one nightmare, plunging its physicality into her new nightmare, as her vaginal opening was being stabbed into and her ribs felt like they were being cracked all over again.

Someone was atop of her.

Celiane snapped awake, defensive, immediately incredulous as her body was being violated yet again. By a policeman again, she saw. This policeman with stripes on his shirt though. A captain? A lieutenant? She couldn't believe this. She started fighting back and was rocked by a vicious backhand. She was stunned and frozen but could only freeze for so long before she used every girl's instinctive last resort of a defense mechanism: She raised her right knee up as fast as she could into his groin and screamed as loud as she could, showing that she was finally fed up with being a victim, while everything in her is screaming in pain.

The policeman immediately folded and she pushed him off of her, off of the bed and onto the dirty floor as a woman in scrubs came rushing in. The same beautiful angelic face from her dream! Nurse Lizi! She immediately began fixing Celiane's sad state and covering her up with the bed sheets, all the while, going on a loud tirade in Spanish on the police captain and even kicking him further, as he still rolled around in agonizing pain on the floor. More people rushed in. More police. More medics.

Celiane was scared even more at the sight of the other police officers, as her experience with police thus far had been all bad: Twice raped and beaten to within an inch of her life. But her fear was never realized as they all payed her very little attention. Instead they listened to the rantings in Spanish from the blue-eyed nurse. They all looked dubious but still followed her directions and got her rapist out of there, leaving Celiane alone with her savior-nurse. Allowing her to feel a momentary safety.

"Thank you for helping-" started Celiane, void of tears and all the way numb to her plight and the brutality of her new reality, before being interrupted.

"You must go! We must get you out of here! Don't you see? They will kill you! Can you move at all?" asked Nurse Lizi.

"I-um, I can try, it just really hurts. All over," said Celiane.

"I know-I know, but these *Policia*, they theenk you kill Manera, so they will kill you! You don' understan?"

"He was raping me, can't I say it's self-defense?" asked Celiane.

"You-you do kill Manera?! These es crazy! How you do such things? He is the most corruption of all of Cien Fuegos *Policia*! These impossible!" said Nurse Lizi as she was ducking into a nearby closet of poorly lit medical bay. She threw some clothes onto the wheelchair she had parked nearby and pushed it over to Celiane. "I was going to help you no matter what, but Manera ... Manera-he rape me at me *Quinceañera Fiesta, Pero*

211

nadir-nobody-believes me because I am but a peasant-and he ES *Policia*, but I happy for you kill him!" She spits on the floor in disgust. "I spit on his dead *Cuerpo-que muerte*-May he rot in hell! Now hurry ... " she adds, walking away as Celiane is attempting to dress in some old, worn out hospital scrubs while favoring her pulverized ribs and sore feet.

Celiane finished dressing and grabbed some yellow hospital 'crocs' styled shoes off of another bed and tried to stand. The pain was almost unbearable, but with her hands on the handles of the wheelchair, pushing it around, she found that she could move about, as long as she was holding onto the wheelchair. She is encouraged. Finally, she is no longer helpless.

As Celiane moved about the room, trying to get the blood moving in her legs so she could get accustomed to walking and to prepare for her escape, she approached the grimy, barely transparent window. The fact that it was painted-shut made no difference once she noted that she was on the second floor and probably wouldn't be able to get far if she had been on the ground floor in her condition. But when she looked through the dirty glass, what she saw made her shiver involuntarily, her fears coming to surface and shaking her.

There were around 10 or 12 men, F.A.R. as well as *Policia*, all surrounding her attempted rapist as he went on animatedly, with his hands and arms waving all around, then ending by his ultimate pointing at the *Policlinico* she was currently hiding safely in. Celiane was suddenly terrified. Her body shuddered in a panic, involuntarily responding to her real fear. At just that moment, the door crashed open, making Celiane almost jump ten feet into the air, despite the pain in her ribs.

Seeing that it was Nurse Lizi bursting through, she sighed in relief, but the look on Lizi's face brought the fear right back to Celiane. Her relief short-lived. "They are coming to kill you! Manera's son demands justice-" started Lizi.

"If they wanted 'justice' they should have killed that bastard themselves long ago ... "

"Es no about that, es about family honor, now come! We must go now!"

"I have nowhere to go-" Celiane started dejectedly.

"Es okay! I have place. You be safe. Come on-" said the nurse as she held out her arm for Celiane to hold onto while she led her to the daunting stairs. Celiane balked at seeing them. "Wait! I can't-" she started to protest.

"*NO HAY ASCENSOR*! We-no-elevator! Let's go!" said a panicking Lizi. It was in that moment where Celiane would come to realize that this nurse was risking her own life to help her, and she decided that she wouldn't allow that to be in vain. She already put her father and his friends in the situation they ended up in, with her bad choices and she would allow nobody else to suffer because of her. She steeled herself and took the first step. She moved.

By the time Celiane and Lizi had made it down the stairs and

213

to the dirt alleyway in the back of the *Policlinico*, Celiane looked pretty bad, her body coated with a sheen of sweat like a horse after the Kentucky Derby race, her body was in obvious anguish.

Confusion clouded her brow, as she was immediately panicked to find that there was no awaiting getaway car to take her away to safety. Incredulity stood prominently on her face as she watched Nurse Lizi toying with something on the side of a red 150cc little motor scooter. "You've got to be kidding me ... " said Celiane in confusion, looking all around nervously.

"Come on, *Americana*! They never catch us on *mi 'Cereza'*, she fastest scooter on whole island," said Nurse Lizi, smiling reassuringly.

Celiane saw no other recourse. She had no other choice but to stay and die, so she pushed herself and climbed on the back as the beautiful Cuban, Nurse Lizi, got the ridiculous little thing started and took off, causing an immediate and all consuming sharp pain to come alive in her ribs again. Celiane had to squeeze her eyes shut, but just before she did, she risked a quick look back and saw several *Policia* come rushing out into the alleyway that they had just hastily vacated. Lizi made a right turn and hit the gas. Celiane could now see what she meant as they weaved in and out of traffic, passing moving cars like they were parked, sitting still.

§§§§

A half an hour later, Lizi thankfully turned into an actual paved alleyway behind another bureaucratic building similar to the *Policlinico* and finally cut off the unbelievable scooter.

"*Ya!* Come on, girl!" said Lizi, grabbing Celiane's hand a little too rough, causing some pain from her ribs to shoot up and making her gasp in desperation. Celiane just pushed her growing apprehension to the side and allowed herself to be pulled along roughly and led inside, to an office styled building with the Cuban flag hanging prominently all throughout the hallways.

"Come on, *Princesa!*" said Lizi, all semblance of her gentleness gone, turned off upon their arrival like a light switch. Celiane continued to allow herself to be drug along the bureaucratic hallways, taking immediate notice to the change in her savior nurse's indifference to her pain and inner torments. She began to feel that maybe something wasn't right.

As Celiane's face grimaced in pain, her eyes barely opened slits, she finally took notice as they approached a massive faux wood and metal desk. The Cuban seal hung behind the desk, along with another Cuban flag, a proud red triangle with a white star and big blue stripes prominent and bright. A severe looking white Cuban girl with blonde hair sat in front of the big bold words, "*Ministerio de interior*".

Celiane once again cursed her choice of taking Creole for the easy A, instead of actually learning a new language by taking

215

Spanish class. Even though she could not actually read the words, and despite Lizi's sudden coldness, Celiane felt somewhat safe just by taking in the seriousness of the surroundings and the cold government looking offices and woman secretary, although she still had a feeling of something off nagging in the back of her conscious. Was it possible that this was some sort of Embassy, Consulate or something like those she had seen in the movies? she asked herself, in between her painful breaths she had been desperately taking. They continued on toward the desk as the blonde woman picked up the phone, saying something into the receiver that Celiane couldn't hear, and couldn't understand if she could.

The blonde turned and nodded at Nurse Lizi as they passed her desk, Lizi still helping a limping Celiane to the closed office door. As Lizi reached out and turned the knob, Celiane happened to glance up and see the name tag on the door and her heart jumped into her throat, her fear immediately etched onto her young and still quite beautiful face. Her nightmare being realized in her new horrible reality. Completely real and unavoidable.

Celiane's whole body stiffened, her mutinous feet refusing to move, complete betrayal showing in her suddenly tearful eyes. NO! she thought to herself, as Lizi opened the door while dragging Celiane along, it can't be!

Celiane glanced into her Savior-Nurse's pretty blue eyes once more, seeing the smile of an evil intent in them, sealing her fate with betrayal and then suddenly and unexpectedly, the floor began rushing up to meet her as she fell. The last thing that she saw, right before her heavy eyelids closed and stole away her vision, was the name tag on the heavy oak door.

Ministerio De Interior

Senor Giancarlos Manera

Celiane passed out again, into a deep and coma-like sleep ...

Chapter Twenty - Three

Wicks, Shelby and Serge sat in the small hut that served as a home for Marta, her husband, and her 7 year old daughter, Catalina. Shelby held Catalina on her lap as they sat in a small love seat in the only other room in the hut besides the bedroom after Catalina had already cried herself to sleep about the dirty *Policia* taking her mother-Marta-in for questioning two days ago. After having hid from the dirty *Policia*, Catalina had been left alone, as her father worked for weeks at a time on a fishing boat, trolling out West Atlantic Ocean nearby Bermuda and there wasn't anyone else to care for her.

When Marty had spoken to some people at a local pool hall, not far from where Wicks and Shelby had suspected Celiane was being kept, he found out the direction she had been headed in and talked to a group of little kids playing who indicated that the *Policia* had busted into this hut and taken two black-complexioned women. After which, they had then come here and found Catalina all alone and hungry, worried to death about her mother.

"We're going to have to split up into two teams, so we can grab Marta and Celiane at once or they might move one or the other ..." said Shelby quietly.

"I know," said Wicks. "And Marty is taking too long with that nurse lady. They should've been back by now." He looked at his tan colored G-Shock again.

Less than five minutes later, EJ, Ty and Marty walked in with

218

a surprise. They had a very pretty white Cuban nurse with the most mesmerizing blue eyes Wicks had ever seen with them. She was zip-tied with her mouth duct-taped shut. Marty was smiling proudly.

"We found this evil little snake-in-the-grass at the *Policlinico* they had kept Celiane at. She was okay until this one kidnapped her and brought her to a representative of the MININT-who also happens to be the father of the Cuban police officer they're saying Celiane had apparently shot and killed. I guess our little Celiane ain't so helpless after all. The intelligence I got from this little devil is that this Manera-a cop-was raping Celiane, she got tired of being a victim and got a hold of his gun and shot him in the head, fleeing from there to here, where the *Policia* were tipped off and she was taken to this blue-eyed devil. She won't give the location up, and believe me, I tried ... " explained EJ.

Wicks got up slowly and deliberately, every bit the look in the form of a menace. "EJ, get that bucket over there and fill it with water. Shelby, can you take this child for a walk while I settle our tab with this nice nurse?" he said, smiling sweetly to Catalina, who automatically smiled back at him, showing that for some strange reason, even with the gold teeth and face tats, Wicks loved kids and has a way with them. He always had.

Shelby stood quietly, motioning Catalina. "C'mon, sweetheart. Let's go for a walk to the store and get you some food."

After they had left, Wicks snatched up the nurse roughly by her beautiful curly hair and slammed her face, still duct-taped, into

219

the bucketful of water, holding it under. After about 20 seconds, he brought her back up and she was desperately trying to yell through the tape.

"MMM! MMMM!" she said, her beautiful blue eyes looking around wildly everywhere, trying to convey her distress, begging for sympathy. There was none to be had. Not from Wicks. He has no sympathy.

Wicks payed her no mind as his team looked on. He just downed her head into the bucket again, his face completely stoic, void of all expressions or even any emotion at all.

"Ah ... hey there, Wicks? Aren't you 'sposed to ask her a question first? Like before you dunk her head in again? At least give her a chance to answer? It's like 'interrogation 101' ... " pointed out Ty.

Still holding her head underwater, Jean blinked his eyes rapidly and then nonchalantly spoke up. "I'm not Wicks. And I'm going to end her life now, so if you are unable to watch, you should leave now ... "

Nobody moved, silently agreeing that it was the justice she so deserved.

Jean brought her head up, right before she could drown, his face a mask, menacing and devoid of all emotion.

"I'm going to remove the tape, if you say a single word other than the location of Celiane, your head doesn't come out of this bucket next time. Understood?" Jean asked her, clenching his teeth, bereft of all empathy for her plight.

"MMMM!" she nodded frantically, thinking that she could still save herself.

Jean ripped the tape off of her mouth roughly while simultaneously unholstering his Sig Sauer P229 from his paddle holster and holding the intimidating gun up to her head. As she tried to gather herself while still on her knees in front of the bucket of water, the spilled water turning to mud on the dirt floor, soaking her light blue clinical scrubs, she looked up into Jean's eyes to see if there was any mercy contained within. She found none. Only a menacing face with an evil smirk on it.

Her eyes widen as she recognizes her own impending doom.

"Please, not kill me! I help her! She in Manera's compound, North of the city and-" started the beautiful nurse, trying and failing to use her pretty face to get what she was so used to getting: Her way.

She was suddenly interrupted by Jean pushing her face back into the bucket of water with his left hand. He quickly brought up his Sig Sauer that was in his right hand and placed it to the back of her head. He then proceeded to place a perfectly centered .40 caliber hollow point through the back of her head, effectively blowing the whole front of her pretty face off and into the water.

As they all stared at the bucket that had been full of clear water, they saw what looked like blood and noodles soup. The greyish brain matter that had exited through the front of her skull began to collect on the surface, looking like grey noodles, along with a perfectly round and beautiful, devilish blue eyeball, morbidly staring upwards at them all in a macabre shock. There would be no facial recognition on this girl.

Silence invaded and conquered the small hut between all of the men present up until Wicks, unaffected by the grisly scene, began issuing orders for them to split up into teams. He reasoned that since EJ, Marty and Serge were all familiar and had worked together in Sandland before, Marty could steal them a car from the Fiat rental place down the street and they would first rescue Marta from the *Policia* building a few blocks over, then meet up at the *Nichardo* pool hall down the street from the hut, where they had began their search at. Catalina would stay in the hut until Wicks, Shelby and Ty rescues Celiane and then pick up Catalina on the way to the pool hall to meet up with Team 2 and Catalina's mother.

§§§§

After EJ, Marty and Serge had left, Wicks and Ty walked quickly to clean up any evidence of the nurse's execution, emptying the bucket behind some trees and putting the once beautiful nurse's body in the bed of the pickup for later disposal.

"Damn, Wicks, you a cold-blooded motherfucker. You would've been a hell of an asset over in Sandland. I've never seen such absence of all emotion before like how you displayed it. I reserve the right to call on you one day," said Ty.

Wicks could only smile.

"You got it ... just remember, I like a challenge ... "

Chapter Twenty - Four

"Man, this is gonna cost you. You're lucky that I had the pleasure of actually dating the coms specialist on the base. Give me a few minutes and I'll see what I can do," said Martinez as he got out of the stolo, a stolen rental Fiat, leaving EJ with Serge as he began dialing on his phone and sliding into the alley to be inconspicuous because he was still wearing Navy SEAL fatigues and didn't want to draw too much attention.

They had left Wicks and Ty to clean up the mess in the hut so that little Catalina wouldn't be exposed to the violence. Jean is EJ's uncle and even EJ had been surprised at the brutality and lack of emotion that his uncle had just displayed while taking the life of that once beautiful blue-eyed nurse. She had been a blue-eyed devil, true enough, but the calmness and lack of emotion that Jean displayed was an even bigger eye opener for EJ. It had actually scared EJ, and he was 'battle tested', Marine action approved.

They were now sitting a block east of the Cien Fuegos *Policia* building and trying to figure a way to get into the place and to get Marta safely out. It was a lot more reinforced than what they had imagined. Also, it was a lot more populated. They hadn't realized when they had first started, how many cops were inside of the building. But just by the size of it, there was no way to attack and rescue Marta with only the three of them. Even corrupt and untrained cops defending a building in high numbers would be able to overtake and defeat them. So, they agreed to allow Marty, who has not only had a lot of experience, but who has spent a lot of time on the island, to come up with an alternate plan, and they would only raid the building as a last resort.

He had come up with the idea of having his friend, who is a communications specialist at Guantanamo Bay Navel Base, call and ask for Marta to be released into U.S. Navel custody. They were quickly shot down-yet another door to corruption was opened. For a certain price of $5,000 American, Cien Fuegos *Policia* would be willing to release her into U.S. Navel custody where she would be able to apply for Asylum Protection, which of course, Ty would be able to pull strings for her and Catalina, as well as her husband to get. It was a small thing Ty could do for her family after they had risked it all to help some American girl they didn't even know.

EJ called Ty and relayed the updated SITREP to him and then explained what was needed. Ty agreed quickly, reminding EJ about those Bitcoin accounts that they had confiscated from the Haitian Sensations lieutenant, Richy Rich and those fanatical muslim terrorists that had ended up blowing EJ out of a second story window and killing 8 of their breach team a couple of years ago with a suicide bomb in Boca Raton. Or had it been a year ago? EJ asked himself. A year and a half maybe? Wow, it seems like forever ago. He thought back to the time ...

Wicks had been following EJ and Ty's target in a terrorism investigation. At the time they hadn't been sure about the relationship between Richy Rich of Haitian Sensations street gang-drug cartel, and the fanatical muslim terrorists he was there meeting with. Once EJ confronted Wicks, he found that Wicks only intended to follow and kill Richy Rich because of the drugs that had been making their way into the hands of kids at the local Youth Center where Wicks and Shelby volunteered at, trying to help the same at risk kids. Needless to say, EJ and Ty arranged a 'disappearing act' for Richy Rich, who it turned out, was only there to exchange his drug proceeds in the form of U.S. currency for the Bitcoins that the terrorists were buying the cash with. Richy Rich was actually here on the Island of Cuba in the Guantanamo Bay black site prison, without even a right to a lawyer. Giving drugs to kids was its own form of terrorism, and Richy Rich would pay for his dirty dealings. Luckily though, they had now found a way to put those evil proceeds to good use-fuck the Congressional Oversight Committee, EJ and Ty knew when and where to use this funding for overall good and didn't need a lot of talk and non-action from Congress.

The $5,000 was payed immediately through the coms specialist friend and they just decided to let Martinez go collect Marta since he speaks fluent Spanish, as well as the fact that he was also still wearing his Navy BCUs, or Battle Combat Uniform, and would be able to solidify the legitimacy of their bribe transaction.

Luckily, the police station was big enough and populated to a point to where hopefully-with all of the traffic coming and going-no one would notice that this Navy SEAL had just walked up to the station without the telltale Navy issued Humvee that they were required to occupy while straying from the base, since they were equipped with a GPS transponder so that the base would know at all times where their soldiers were located and could respond to that location immediately if there was ever any trouble. But nobody ever strayed as far as Cien Fuegos, because on top of being particularly unfriendly to Americans, it was also a long drive and there would be no reason for them to ever go there anyway. Until now, and this was a main reason EJ had told Marty, "No HumVee", because when all of these bodies start dropping, and there would definitely be a lot of bodies to be dropped, then when the clean up began and nobody wanted any evidence of an American presence being left behind, they couldn't have a GPS footprint, tagging them right in the middle of a conflict.

They didn't need anything leading back to them or to the Navel Base.

Once they collected Marta and explained their plan to her from Team 1 going to rescue Celiane all the way to Ty's intention to offer her and her family asylum in America in exchange for her help in saving Celiane-as they all knew the risks that Marta could face because of her help and knowing exactly how a communist country would be reacting to what it sees as a betrayal or treasonous acts-she flat out refused their offer. She had no intention of ever leaving or betraying her beloved Island of Cuba.

She explained to them that the *Policia* had only taken her because of a bribe by the operator of a local brothel on the Eastside of town had wanted to be able to interrogate her further into the whole situation with Celiane and how she had gotten involved with her. She explained that the cops or *Gobierno*, had no interest in her beyond getting more of a bribe out of her. Since the Americans had payed her bribe, she was more than grateful, but she would just like to return home to her daughter and to be left alone. They continued to try to convince her for a while, but seeing the futility of further argument, EJ made the call to just drop her at the hut and to get directions to Senor Manera's house located North of the city and to head there to provide backup for Team 1, everything having worked out so far for them, they wanted to keep the successful operations going.

Chapter Twenty - Five

Once Wicks had readily agreed to be of later assistance to Ty-a favor for a favor-in turn, the Agency, Ty had begun to pull out all the stops with one of his own assets in logistics that he is able to call in favors to. By using his sat phone to coordinate the attack, Ty's logistics expert had given them the layout and everything save the actual blueprints, to the compound of Senor Manera, *Ministerio De Interior*. They had all of the necessary details to conduct a successful raid.

There were patrol guards, gate guards, and ten foot walls topped with broken glass bottles, the Cuban version of razor wire. It was going to be a difficult task, but after all Wicks has been through, in addition to Shelby's police training and experience and Ty's Special Forces training before his time at the Agency, this should be a breeze for them to put together and accomplish.

Just then, after finishing getting Catalina settled, Shelby jumped into the front seat of the cab in the stolo truck, forcing Wicks into the middle seat. "She'll be alright till we get back ... " Shelby said as they pull off into the quickly darkening dusk of the evening.

"EJ and them already called and the dirty pigs only want five racks to get Marta back. I gave them the money in a Bitcoin transfer, so it should be done fairly quick, and without drawing the attention of the *Policia*-as we are surely about to do with this raid ... " said Ty, leaving the rest of the obvious unsaid. They all knew and had agreed on the risks being involved in order to save Celiane from this hell and bring her home to her family. They were all in.

As they made the drive in silence, Ty was all nervous energy and the word vomit began its ascent into the truck's interior. "You ever listen to these socialist news reporters lately? I heard what they called "Climate Philosophy" the other day and-" started Ty.

"What the fuck is Climate Philosophy?" asked Wicks in an uninterested monotone, interrupting Ty.

"That's my fuckin' point here, Wicks," said Ty. "The fucking guy was interviewing some kind of expert in his scientific field, and this stupid-genius was saying that if we were going to freeze to death or were like those people on the Titanic could have done, all we have to do to survive is to eat a lot of hot sauce and jalapeños-they will make you sweat and heat your body and then-"

"Hold on!" interrupted Shelby. "Are you being serious right now? Or is this how you Agency folks find humor to loosen up before a mission?"

"Don't worry baby, he grows on ya ... " said Wicks, surprising himself with the admission.

"Nah, I'm being serious right now! These ass clowns think they're going to save us-and the planet-with electric cars and jalapeño sauce ... " Ty trailed off, but then added as an afterthought, "I mean, I know it's just random-and yea, we do tend to lighten up the mood before missions, but these are the ass clowns that are now running our country's government and our mainstream media. It's just sad, ya know? This is who we fought so hard over for so long in Sandland. That is our legacy. That's what we leave for our kids ... "

Silence filled the truck's interior for a few minutes before Shelby finally spoke up. "I do have one question for ya, Ty ... "

"Sure, anything," said Ty, now hoping for some input on his political current events conversation, after thinking nobody was interested in it.

"What in God's name is an 'Ass Clown'?" she asked, smiling mischievously.

Wicks finally allowed his gangsta facade to slip as he couldn't help but to break into laughter, until he saw Ty's serious facial expression as the truck slowed.

They had finally reached their destination. Ty pulled the truck to the side of the road and into some bushes to try to conceal their vehicle's presence, allowing them to keep the element of surprise and avoid alerting the target enemy prematurely.

"Holy shit, it's big," said Ty in awe at the beautiful colonial-styled mansion. "We are definitely going to need to split up to take this place quietly, cause I sure didn't bring any suppressors, did you?"

"Nah," said Wicks. "It's all good, we can improvise. We can take as many as we can in silence with our K-Bar knives, then at first sound of a discharge, we can go 'weapons free' until we get her out of there. What about Coms?"

"All good," added Shelby. "I'll merge-call both of you and we can use our Bluetooth earpiece to commun-"

"What about cell towers or satellites?" asked Wicks, learning, but still not yet fully up to date on technology, since he had been in prison for over 13 years, so he is always erring on the side of caution.

"Won't matter," said Ty. "If we're not gone by the time there's an investigation, then it's cause we failed and we're dead ... "

"Nah-we ain't finna let Celiane down like that. We the only chance she got and I won't let her down," said Wicks vehemently, heart filled with enough passion to take on the whole army of F.A.R. soldiers. His determination is contagious, as Shelby and Ty both nodded sincerely in agreement, silently pledging their lives to save Celiane from the comic-book-like super villain who had taken her for his own revenge.

"We'll get her, bae," said Shelby, with her gentle reassurance. "How about I take the front gate guard? Wicks-left side wall, Ty-right side?"

"It's a plan. Weapons free-leave nothing breathin'. Let's go drop some bodies," replied Ty, pulling his ski-mask down over his face and charging a round into the chamber of his rifle. Wicks followed suit and went to work, doing what he does best.

Chapter Twenty - Six

When Celiane awoke from her worst dreams imaginable, she realized that her reality was an even worse nightmare than even the one on Elm Street that Freddy Krueger could possibly impose. She was instantly terrified and almost completely sure she was going to die. She also knew she wasn't going down without a fight. A brawl actually. She refuses to be a victim anymore. She took a look around the dark room as she tried futilely to move her arms and legs but sensed that she was tied down on some sort of table.

It was an altar-she finally realized in a panic. This fucking maniac had her tied down to a fucking altar with candles lit everywhere around her creating an even more ominous and scary dimness to the dark room. Next to her was a dark shape that she has at first missed in the dim light, but upon further inspection, she determined it was a naked man. Looking even closer she could see the perfect, yet tiny hole in between his eyes. Celiane finally lost her shit. It was the rapist pig that she'd killed.

"OH MY GOD! OH MY GOD! OH MY GOD! OH MY GOD! OH MY GOD!" mumbled Celiane repetitively in complete shock and terror as she began tearing and ripping at the twine binds holding her ankles and wrists to the altar securely. She continued to beg God as she kept looking desperately around, in a state of complete and utter horrified panic. A voice suddenly reached her ears.

"*No te precupes*-it's all going to work out for the best! *La*

Santa muerte-she gonna make right all of your evil ... *No te precupes*..." said the insane looking MININT officer, trailing off as he is stepping out of the dark shadows. He-who had been the smiling face that her traitor nurse had handed her over to in the second most painful display of betrayal that Celiane had ever in her life experienced. After all she had been through and the betrayal she had experienced, even she hadn't seen that one coming. Nurse Lizi had effectively deceived her and then successfully turned her over to the same people who now wanted her dead. Or rather, whatever the ridiculous set up was, it might even be worse than death. Although, only one thing could be worse than death to her, and that was a life living in that hell of a brothel.

As he was walking out, Celiane continued her frantic look all around, desperately trying to uncover anything that could be of use to aid her in her escape or at worse, her defense. She noticed the entire room is painted black, the ceiling a dark maroon. There was a large mural of a hooded figure, *La Santa Muerte*, Celiane assumed. It was surrounded by small offerings of food and liquor. There was money and a lot of jewelry, as well as other things ... stranger things.

Celiane started when she realized that she and her rapist were both positioned directly underneath this mural, and both of them were surrounded by candles and eerie symbols and designs. Shit! She realized that she must be some kind of a sacrifice or an offering as well-into some sadistic ritual shit this fuck had conjured up in the deep confines of his mentally insidious and savage mind. She kept looking around and then finally her eyes set themselves upon a small wheeled metal cart-like table next to the altar that she was lying on. Sitting on the table next to an ancient looking book, opened to what she thought was most likely some sort of incantation for whatever weird and evil ritual this was, there was a large ancient and ritualistic looking knife. It was black with red and maroon designs all along the handle and it had all kinds of inscriptions all over the curved blade and a big black stone on the bottom of its handle, surrounded by small red stones. She knew she could try to get this knife. She would have to, since she saw no other option.

If she moved her left foot a little bit, she could just touch it. The only problem is: what then? Even if she could move the table right next to her, with tied hands she couldn't pick the knife up or use it. She sighed in misery and just keeps struggling against her binds. She would not give up, she would fight until her last breath because she was done with being a victim.

The madman that had set all this up came back in and began to mess with the book. Finding the correct page, she assumed, he then began reading in a whisper at first. Celiane was steadily pulling and pushing against her twine restraints. The madman was mumbling spells or incantations, she figured. He was starting to get louder and louder as he got into his own world. She felt the sharp bite of the twine, working itself into the skin in all of her limbs. She could feel she is bleeding, but she would be damned if she just lay there again and be a victim in the middle of Cuba. Her mind is set.

235

So, she tugged and pulled on her now bloody restraints. The blood had soaked into the twine, possibly helping to ease them a bit as she was starting to feel some give in the bindings on her right arm.

The pain was something she had grown used to. It is something that would never hold Celiane back again. She no longer feared pain. That is not it. It was-not getting out of here and being able to tell her brothers and parents exactly how much she loved and appreciated them-that scared her. Not getting her dad out of jail and home safely scared her. Pain would never scare her. Fear would never rule over her. Never again.

So, she continually worked her twine restraints, starting to feel some give in all of her limbs and she felt a modicum of hope spring up into her spirit. She was going to get out of this shit and home to her family or she was going to die trying. She would no longer be anyone's victim. She had already accepted that her potential saviors, Wicks and Shelby, had given up on tracking her down since she had missed the rendezvous and been moved so many times it would be impossible to find her. But she still believed that she could and would get out of this. She would fight until her last dying breath, she knew this. She would accept her fate, sure. But only after she had fought until her death that she knew might be coming. Only then would she accept whatever her fate was.

She is now resolved. Determined. She isn't a victim anymore-she is a fighter and she will fight with her last breath, her last burst of energy. She continued struggling with her bonds, determined to get free. To fight. Then-

BOCKA!

Suddenly, the whole dynamic changed. Her world changed with the sound of that first shot. She looked at the madman's face and recognized the confusion contained therein-heard his anxiety and fear when he spoke.

"What-*QUIEN ESTA* ... ?" he started.

But then soon after, there were more shots. Many more. Celiane's right hand came free finally and she immediately began freeing her left hand. The hand closest to the table with the ritual knife on it. The knife she could free her legs with. The knife that she would soon use to kill the madman with, ending it all.

Chapter Twenty - Seven

Shelby felt her man's determination, and inside of herself, she felt just as determined to have Wicks' back as she was to save Celiane. She felt almost like she was Celiane. They were both Haitian girls whom had grown up as outsiders in the South Florida slums while trying to fit in with the American black *Yanke'e* community and being made fun of because of their meager upbringings and humble, yet strict values and morals in their households growing up. Shelby had indeed been where Celiane was at in her struggle to fit in, so she can sincerely relate with Celiane and understand how she could have fallen in this trap she was now in.

"We'll get her, bae," Shelby had said with her gentle reassurance. "How about I take the front gate guard? Wicks-left side wall, Ty-right side?"

"It's a plan. Weapons free-leave nothin' breathin'. Let's go drop some bodies," replied Ty, before pulling his ski-mask down over his face then charging a round into the chamber of his rifle.

Shelby noticed that Wicks only nodded imperceptibly, as if to himself. She had been noticing a changing dynamic between Wicks and Jean lately. It was starting to bother her. Dating a dual personality in one body is stressful and hard enough. She definitely didn't need any complications to add to the equation. She had to set that aside for now though and get her head back in the game. She couldn't afford distractions right before action.

They split up, Wicks cutting left, Ty doubling back to go to the right side, and Shelby just got on the main road, heading toward the guard gate. From about 100 feet away, she saw the two guards. One big, black and young. The other, a slightly tanned older and compact built man. Both are dressed in a grey paramilitary outfit with ancient-looking revolvers on their belts. They should have noticed her walking in their direction but had failed to do so thus far. She knew she couldn't chance any noise until Wicks and Ty had gotten in place, so 20 feet short of the guard booth, she dumped her pack and weapons. She would make good use of her Krav Maga training she had trained for years to learn with her Israeli ex-Mossad friend, Gal, training hard in the Miami Gardens underground gym they both had a membership to.

As she approached the guard gate, she slowed her walk and began to sway her hips in a way that she knew would get the two Cuban guards' attention. When she arrived, she saw that her intentions had been well received, as she smiled invitingly to the men whose complete attention was on nothing other than her swaying hips in her skin-tight black skinny jeans and black sports bra. She had them both speechless and lost. She closed the last few steps of distance as quickly as she could while she had them mesmerized, setting the proper distance for her preemptive strike.

"*Y quien eres* ... ?" the small one began, still in a daze and not seeing the honey trap she had set for him.

Shelby said nothing but wasted no time in her offensive attack.

She had approached and positioned herself with the small guy on her right, and the big one to the left. She immediately struck out at the big one's throat with a snap jab, hard in his Adam's apple, wrecking the cartilage and causing his hands to automatically reach for his neck, putting him out of commission for the foreseeable future while she turned her attention to the smaller of the two. Just as fast, he was lunging towards her with his right hand reaching out to grab her. She quickly grabbed his hand, bent the wrist in, and turned her body into his personal space. She then pulled his arm into her chest while dropping all of her body weight low and forward. She flipped him over her left shoulder and onto the ground in front of her with her body's momentum, quickly pivoting and pulling his arm-still in her grip-in between her thighs while wrapping her legs around his neck and squeezing until the man's neck was snapped, no longer capable of drawing breath or even able to defend himself. He dies quickly.

She then hurried to get up to bring her attention back to the other one who was still struggling and holding his throat with one hand while trying to get up off the ground with the other. She hit him with a flying knee as he got almost level with her chest. His nose broke, creating a blood faucet-and adding to his distress, as he could now neither breathe through his mouth or nose, promising him a very terrible and horrifying end. A slow and painful death.

Shelby was already dragging the body of the smaller dead guard back to the booth as the bigger guard was laying there dying and committing that last image -of her dragging his partner-into his soon-to-be erased memory banks. By the time she had returned in order to drag his big body to the guard booth to hide, he had already expired, his soul slowly leaving his body as his bodily functions had relaxed, releasing his bladder and bowels as well.

After disposing of her two victims' bodies in the guard booth, she ran back and got her weapons and pack, before committing to the path down the drive. She then manually opened the 15 foot metal gates that stood backing the entrance road. She began walking down the drive, observing all of the beautiful thick growth of trees and shrubs located on and taking up most of the square acreage of this compound. Her instinct was telling her she needed to make sure nobody could escape down this drive if Wicks and Ty had already began their offensive, but as she got about a quarter mile up the drive, she saw Ty just coming out of the jungle of trees, his black clothes looking wet as if he had been swimming. He quickly took notice of her and lowered his Colt model AR-15, jogging over to her as they continued to follow the drive together.

Upon further observation of Ty's black attire, Shelby concluded that his clothes were in fact just soaked in blood, and not water, as she had originally suspected. "You good?" she asked him, her brows raised in concern.

"Just peachy," he said, looking down at his own appearance. "It's not mine, I disposed of their roaming patrol. We're good ... and Wicks?" Shelby touched her Bluetooth earpiece, activating it and connecting her to the open phone line with her man. "Bae? You good?" she asked quietly, as they turned the last curve in the road, placing them in full view of the mansion.

"All good, bae. I'm going in the back door now ... " answered

Jean. "Okay, me and Ty are coming up on the front of the house now-"

BOCKA!

It happened so fast. All in a split second it had popped off. A guard had been smoking a cigarillo and saw them coming, quickly reaching for his ancient AK-47 that was leaning up against the nearby tree. Ty was lightning quick in his reflexes bringing up his AR-15 and placing a perfectly centered round into his target's forehead. There goes their element of surprise ...

Chapter Twenty - Eight

His thoughts on rerun in his mind, while already bleeding and pretty fucking pissed about it, Wicks continued through the dense forest surrounding the mansion almost every inch of the whole compound. Upon his scaling of the ten foot wall topped with broken glass, he had cut his thigh pretty deep on his left leg. He was kind of pissed because it was unprofessional and embarrassing. He should've been more careful. So, after an internal battle between he and Jean, Wicks relented, letting Jean be front and center, finally believing that he was ready. Wicks felt guilty-he should have never allowed Jean to kill that nurse. He had opened a door that had been closed since Jean had killed a man trying to molest him at the tender age of 13. But Jean hadn't actually killed Tavares, had he? No, Wicks had been conceived and born and the responsibility had been completely left at his feet. Him being the violent one.

Ultimately they used an aluminum baseball bat and had completely and unceremoniously bashed Tavares' head in, exposing his brain matter and leaving him for dead. It was at this point-that Wicks was no longer Jean's nickname. Wicks and Jean had split. Ever since then, and at every chance he got, Wicks would beat up and kill a 'chomo', or child molester. He enjoys this work because he himself was almost abused, so in each chomo he had killed over the years, he felt that he was saving another kid from being abused-stopping the cycle as it were. But where does it leave him now? he asked himself rhetorically. "You can't ask yourself rhetorical questions, remember?" said Jean ironically. "It defeats the purpose of being rhetorical ... "

Shit is getting worse, they can both agree on that. A sharp pitter patter and a bark could be heard coming closer and closer. Jean pulled out his K-Bar knife, knowing Wicks and everyone had agreed on silence until they had eyes on Celiane. Her safety was always going to be everyone's first priority for sure. He began to hear a rustle in the foliage and prepared himself, but nothing could prepare him for the size of the pitbull. It was almost as tall as his hip, running right at him. Heavy too. Maybe 130 pounds or even more. Jean held his K-Bar in his right hand, so he offered the dog his left forearm horizontally, protecting his vitals and yet giving the dog something to latch onto.

The dog took the bait, immediately jumping up, its enormous jaws like those of a gator, unimaginably powerful-locking on to his forearm and its weight pulling Jean's whole body downward. Jean carefully and humanely slides his K-Bar blade into the large neck behind the jaws that are so powerfully attached to his arm. He slides it left and then right-in a quick succession, severing the main arteries in the attack dog's neck, killing him almost instantaneously.

The dog's almost imperceptible whimper was quick and instantly cut off as soon as his throat was severed, and Jean was sure it hadn't been heard. Such a damn shame, thought Jean. He loves dogs, loves Pits, but a dog is only as good as his master trains him to be, so the silence of this one was a regrettable-but necessary casualty. He continued on from there.

As he came closer to the mansion, Jean could see two guards smoking their cigarellos and not really paying attention to their surroundings. He saw a bald one and a medium built one with a pony tail. They were there just conversing, laughing even.

Jean keeps going until he was about 15 feet from the back entrance to the house, passing another huge building that looks to be an airplane hanger or warehouse. He ignores it and concentrates on the backdoor and the guards in front of the door. Probably the kitchen entrance, he thought, looking intently at the door they were standing in front of. He contemplated his next move and came up with a plan to take out both guards silently, before they were able to up their ancient Russian made AK-47 rifles. He took off his pack as silently as he could and grabbed his still bloody K-Bar. He then picked up a small rock and tossed it over their heads and heard it hit the bush right next to the farthest guard, the bald one, perfectly executing his distraction technique.

At the noise, both guards turned to look and see what was in the bushes. Jean sprung into action. With his K-Bar knife up and at the ready, a cool and relaxed confidence in his demeanor-provided by Wicks-Jean snatched the closest guard with his back turned to him by his Antonio Banderas look-a-like pony tail and slid the K-Bar across his throat, opening up a fountain of blood. Hearing the gurgling sound of his dying partner, the baldheaded guard was bringing up his weapon as he turned back toward his pony-tailed friend just in time to have his entire face and chest painted red by the splash of the sudden blood fountain.

Jean, being behind Ponytail, was spared the blood works that the open carotid artery assaulted the other guard with, so he could still see perfectly. Baldy, on the other hand, was blinded by the blood and hesitated just long enough for Jean to stop him. Jean slid his finger inside the trigger guard, but behind the trigger, jamming it to block Baldy from pulling his trigger and alerting others to their presence. With Jean yanking the trigger towards him, the man's body, still tightly gripping the Ak47's stock, was also inadvertently pulled toward Jean violently.

Jean used the leverage of pulling the AK-and in turn the attached body of Baldy-to bring up his other hand and plunge the K-Bar straight into Baldy's chest as he looked into his eyes at the registered panic and surprise in his face. The force and violence that Jean had used displayed his overall power and inner strength when he forced the whole K-Bar, all the way to the hilt, through Baldy's chest plate and straight into his heart, splitting the organ into two distinct and separate parts, ending his life as if turning off a light switch.

Jean quickly grabbed his K-Bar, pulling it out of Baldy's chest and replacing it into his sheath on his belt after wiping the access blood on Baldy's uniform. He took another look, admiring his handiwork. Proud of himself, seeing he can do it just as good as Wicks can. He snapped out of it though, keeping his head in the game and remembering that it was Celiane's life that was really on the line. He grabbed a leg in each hand, one leg from each guard, and began dragging them back behind the bushes he had thrown the stone in. He made quick work of it, and although there was nothing he could do about the splashed blood all over the steps, he was now ready to move into the mansion through this kitchen door. He ran and got his pack and rifle, not even considering picking up one of the ancient and rusty AK-47s. His Kel-Tec RDB Defender and the extended 50 round magazine filled with NATO green tip rounds had been tried and had already proved to be a superb weapons system many times over, so he stuck with what he knew and threw the AKs into the bushes with the bodies, after removing both of the magazines and throwing them as far as he could. He then dug into his pack real quick to take care of his bleeding thigh and forearm before he began to lose too much blood. There weren't any serious arteries hit, but he needed to stop the bleeding just the same.

After wrapping up his bleeding wounds tightly, he brought up his rifle and turned the door knob to the back door, finding it unlocked.

"Bae? You good?" he heard Shelby asking in his ear.

"All good, bae. I'm going in the back door now ... " He started to push the door open to enter the mansion.

"Okay, me and Ty are coming up on the front of the house now-"

BOCKA!

Jean immediately panicked, speaking louder than he had intended. "Shelby, bae? Are you okay? Are you-" he started loudly, before she answered him, interrupting his panicky pleas for her answers, finally reassuring him, explaining her status and what had happened from her end.

Just then though, apparently hearing his loud voice as he had already had the back door almost all the way open, another guard came into the what he now knew was the service entrance. Jean upped his Kel-Tec Defender and pulled his trigger, set to three round bursts, watching as the guard did almost a perfect back flip when the three green tip .223 rounds hit one after another, center mass on his target, as if Jean was born for this kind of fire fight, this deadly combat, even without Wicks in control.

With the cat out of the bag and everyone in and around this house now aware of their presence and the attack, Jean keeps his gun up in a firing position and keeps it pushing. He follows through the same door the guard had emerged from, stepped over his already dead body and entered the large, yet sparsely furnished kitchen. Seeing no targets, he pushed on through the double swinging doors and entered into a big, cavernous living room. He scanned it quickly and visually cleared it with his Kel-Tec still up and in a firing position, ready for all possible action.

Moving on in a light jog, he found himself faced with a choice. He had to decide if he should follow a long and red carpeted hallway, or to take the royal staircase. The stairs are wide and beautifully decorated with a big tapestry on the wall and red decorative carpet lining the stairs in the center. He chose the stairs and quickly ascended to the top, knowing that every second after the first shot, counted down time left on the clock of Celiane's life and limited their ability to be able to rescue her.

Jean automatically follows his first instinct and bypasses the first three single door rooms and goes for the big vaulted double door room instead, having a specific feel that this doorway was leading to something grand, being how the vaulted walls and ceilings indicated something, not to mention all of the designs and symbols all over the doors themselves.

He could hear a girl's voice and a man's shouting in a mixture of accented English and Spanish, so he knew this had to be the right room. He got ready to kick the doors down but paused for a second, mentally calling for Wicks to come forward to take over. "C'mon, Wicks! C'mon! C'mon! C'mon!" Finally, his eyes began to blink rapidly, Wicks coming forth and taking over.

"I know, Jean. I feel ya. But you can do this. You don't need me anymore. We are one and the same. You won't let Celiane down. C'mon, let's go save her, together-let's get it!" Wicks says, steeling himself, lifting his Kel-Tec up into a firing position, he shifted his weight back and rushed forward, kicking at the heavy double doors. The incredibly strong doors held, so Wicks backed up and ran full speed, slamming his whole body weight into the doors, finally breaking the lock in between them and gaining entrance finally. As he was bursting through the doors, several shots were fired in his direction in a rapid succession, forcing him to move fast.

BOC! BOC! BOC! BOC! BOC!

Wicks hit the ground and rolled with his already gained

momentum, but he still felt the shock and jerk of being hit. Everything went numb because of the adrenaline, but he had felt the acute pain in his shoulder and also in his hip somewhere.

BOC! BOC! BOC!

He was definitely hit, but as the madman fired a few more shots with his Russian made Makarov automatic, Wicks was safely behind a cement column and tried to assess his wounds. He felt a sharp pain in his hip. Looking down he saw he was leaking through his lower back on the side as well as his hip. Through, and through. It wasn't so bad. He must have been shot through the door and the heavy wood had slowed the bullet's velocity down, lessening the damage.

"You come for this *chonga*, ey? She kill my son-Enrique, now, *La Santa muerte* will bring him back for me in her body-"

Wicks peeked out leading with his Kel-Tec and fired two pulls of the three round bursts. But even though he hadn't hit anything, he learned both the madman, and Celiane's positions. The MININT officer was standing dead center in front of the mural on the wall, which after all his time in prison, he knew to be a depiction *La Santa muerte*. Some damn vodoo shit, he thought to himself.

"I ain't come to talk, *cabron*!" said Wicks, trying to distract as he rolled out from behind the pillar and started firing again.

TA TA TAT! TA TA TAT! TA TA TAT!

His three round bursts hit the mural and all of those sacrificial-vodoo-looking offerings in front of it. The madman was ducking behind Celiane each time Wicks fired and was now screaming like a wild animal, realizing his ritual was ruined, completely losing control of himself.

"NOOO! What have you-" he started as he stood up, intending to save his mural, or the sacrifices to it, yet was rudely interrupted by Wicks. Or by Wicks sending a bunch of green tips his way- better yet.

It was just the opening Wicks had been waiting on. He ran out toward the madman and let off a burst of fire, immediately hitting his target in the high upper chest area. He lost his balance as he was trying to aim his Makarov pistol, which caused him to fall forward, right toward Celiane, who was struggling to get free from her bounds.

Wicks was still moving in the direction of his target , gun up in a firing position. Just as he had locked on and was about to fire another three round burst, the unbelievable happened. Wicks froze, disbelief written all over his face.

Celiane had somehow gotten a hold of a mean looking knife and when the corrupt MININT was distracted by Wicks and close enough to her, she plunged the knife over and over, deep into his chest and neck, ending it all while ending him and his psychotic break with reality. Wicks was definitely impressed. Celiane has proven herself to be a fighter. A real survivor.

He ran up quickly, never letting his guard down. He saw the madman's blank and lifeless eyes, unbelieving, staring upward to the heavens, yet seeing nothing.

"I killed him! I killed him! I killed-" Celiane was softly

repeating the phrase over and over, clearly traumatized by the whole experience.

TA TA TAT!

Wicks put three .223 rounds into the crazy man's head. He wanted Celiane to be able to sleep at night, and both Wicks and Jean knew what a traumatic experience the taking of a life was.

"No, Celiane. I killed him. It's all over now, 'lil mama. Let's get you out of here and back to your family. It's over now-"

"No! It's not over!" she snapped. "I need to go back for the other girls-I can't just-" Celiane started, trying to demand.

"We can't! We just attacked a government official! We can't just ... " Wicks tried to reason with her, but with one look into her eyes as he was untying her feet, he knew he would go and get her friends for her.

"Okay, ma. C'mon. Let's go and get 'em ... "

Chapter Twenty - Nine

The memory of Celiane's version of events were a little bit different from her point of view. She heard more attacking gunshots coming from outside and the return fire sound effects of a real live gun battle going on. It's got to be Wicks and Shelby, her potential rescuers, though she could see no reason it could be them. Who else could be starting a whole live raid on a high ranking government official in a third world communist country though? she asks herself silently as she is living in her pain, not hating the pain, yet still maintaining her control of the continuous manufacture and development of the pain. She is concentrating so hard, on not only her pain, but also on the battle against her twine restraints. Pulling, tugging-pushing her hand back and forth, her own blood as the lubrication for loosening her other hand. And then her feet. Then the knife. She sees it clearly on the table. Ready to be taken-to be used. By her. On him. He is a whole different breed of evil-but Celiane is going to kill him.

Back and forth she went. Looser and easier. Nothing else in the world mattered. She jumped a little bit when this crazy motherfucker next to her started shooting at the door as it burst open and in a blur, a man ran and ducked behind the pillar and fired a few shots. But other than that, she was completely oblivious to all that was going on around her. All she knew-all she cares about, is getting her left hand free, getting to this knife, and then fighting for her life. She was no longer a victim. She will never again be a victim. She is a fighter. She just started getting it really loose, using both hands to fight the knots in the twine.

There were a few shouts, few gunshots and some screaming. She heard that all at the same time, yet as she continues to tug and pull, it seems as though time is standing still. She knows Wicks was hit, but she also knows that he didn't come alone as she hears other guns being fired, further away. Shelby. The cop lady. Wicks' girlfriend. Such a strange couple, she thinks to herself, but then suddenly, her left hand almost breaks free as one of the twines broke through. She froze, disbelief and elation raising to the surface in her emotions at the same time. But it only lasted for a moment, and then she snapped out of her daze. She worked at freeing her left hand, knowing she needed her left in order to get the knife on the table and then she would be able to free her legs and kill this man-demon. This sick monster of a man.

Working her left hand just a little bit more, she got her final wish, freeing her left hand. She immediately reached for the ritualistic knife, knowing she's got just the right ritual for this creepy motherfucker. Wanting to-no-needing to kill him.

Screaming and stabbing, she blacks out. It's almost as if she is standing back and watching somebody else murder her captor- taking his life and serving up proper justice, like it isn't Celiane herself, stabbing repetitively all about his throat and chest. Somebody else giving this monster what he most certainly has coming. No, before all this happened, Celiane could never even hurt a fly. She's a fighter now and she is definitely going to hurt this fly, because stabbing him 28 times has no doubt, finally killed him. He isn't going to survive what the not-Celiane person, outside of Celiane's body, has done to him. No doubt about what his fate or even his mortality is, she begins to repeat a phrase over and over, certain of being responsible for this life being taken by her hands. No more victim. Only a surviver and a fighter. She is alive ... he is not. She is no longer a victim-he is just no longer ...

"I killed him! I killed him! I killed-" she was saying as if in a spell. Wicks woke her quickly though.

TA TA TAT!

Wicks blew his brains all over the floor and she has no doubt about his being dead now. He was saying something about it 'being over', but this could never be over. Not while Tip still existed and the other girls were still being abused in that place. That hell. Celiane quickly convinced Wicks to go back for her friends, even though he had only come for her, she could never leave those girls to that kind of fate, that type of abuse. Nobody deserves a life like that. It was misery, no kind of life at all. A factual hell.

As he was helping her down from the altar, Shelby and another man came running in, guns up and at the ready. Just a tad bit late to the party after having cleared the rest of this hell hole, she assumed.

"Celiane! C'mon, let's get you out of here and home to your family," Shelby said, holding Celiane by her waist to support her movement.

Ty immediately took point, glad to be leaving after obtaining

255

their objective, leading them out of the room and then down the stairs where they surprisingly found EJ, Marty, and Serge. Celiane took in the looks on all their faces and registered the seriousness, and even fear, displayed therein. But what really took precedence, is the determination that they all shared, dominating all of their collective facial expressions.

"The *Policia* and F.A.R. are all headed this way, we gotta find a way out the back way to get outta here," said EJ. "Follow me!"

"But it's all jungle out back, " said Wicks. "I came in that way, shit."

"We can't shoot it out with 'em, Unk! There's just too many of 'em ... " said EJ.

"Fuck it, I did see a building back there, maybe it's got something we can use, let's go!" said Wicks. "Y'all go ahead and lead the way. I'm going to cover our back trail." He took off up the stairs as Shelby led Celiane out the back door following EJ and Serge, while Ty and Martinez brought up the rear, almost slipping on the blood that Wicks left pooled up on the back steps outside the exit door.

They had just made it to a hanger-type building when Celiane heard some gun shots and watched as a fire was just beginning to spread out on the top floor. She saw that Wicks had crawled out of the window and was climbing down the branch of a nearby tree that had luckily been growing close enough to the window for him to grab a hold of. After a second passed, she could no longer see him, as they had finally made it inside of the cavernous hanger, made up of a crazy and exclusive inventory of unique rides.

Looking around, she saw all kinds of old and exotic restored cars. Most of which she had never seen before, but two of them she did recognize. One was a tank, and it had what looked like old Russian markings on it from the USSR. The other was a 1950's Cadillac convertible. There were also some dirt bikes and four wheelers present, amongst other random things, one of which looked to be a home-made submarine? she wondered to herself, taking a fascinating look at the blimp looking machine.

As her rescuers talked amongst themselves for a minute, she admired the Cadillac. It was definitely a beautiful car. Candy apple red. It reminded her of Bella. Then of Sweets, of whom she had a lot of mixed feelings about. She finally had to confront and accept the fact that he is dead. That had been Tip's intention all along in order for her to take control of all the girls. Celiane was going to put a stop to that plan though. She would save them as Wicks and Shelby had come to save her.

§§§§

The one who they called Martinez was staying behind just long enough to draw attention away from their escape. The rest of them were coupling together on four-wheelers and dirt bikes to get away. They had left one for Martinez to follow behind them, but he had told them he was a Navy SEAL, and as a rule, they never take the path of least resistance. They always take the battle to the enemy-whether in stealth or head on battle, so he was going towards the battle to give the rest of them time to escape.

"Hey, Marty," shouted Ty. "You sure you know how to operate that shit?"

"I mean, sure. How hard could it be?" asked Martinez, as he was climbing onto the tank, admiring the soviet relic, painted green, yet its rusty color shining through.

"Well, maybe not maneuvering, but you definitely still gonna need a weapons officer to operate the heavy guns, you can't drive and shoot," said Ty smiling.

"And you're volunteering?"

"Sure, I don't see why not, they've got Serge with them-who can hot-wire anything with a motor-and I can find my own ride once we get back to base, so why wouldn't I go for a lil adventure?" asked Ty, still smiling with his good humor.

"Well, welcome aboard, Chief Sergeant Weapons Specialist."

"I don't mind if I do ... " said Ty, now climbing up on the tank just as troops started running towards the hanger, ready to initiate their offensive attack.

"Shelby-Wicks, it was fun, can't wait till our next mission! Remember the jalapeños! EJ, Serge! See you on the other side!" said Ty, saluting them before finally ducking his head inside and closing the hatch behind him, the tank taking off, crashing through the 20 foot hanger doors. Gun fire could easily heard immediately. Then huge booms began to overpower the small arms fire as Ty was manning the 50mm long barreled cannon, blowing holes in the framework of the house big enough for the tank to pass through.

"What was that he said about jalapeños?" asked EJ as he, Shelby and Wicks got on the dirt bikes, all being experienced riders. Serge got on a four-wheeler, Celiane quickly got on the back, holding on for dear life.

"Just something that the 'ass clowns' were talking about ... " said Shelby, laughing as she revved up her bike and hit it into first gear, taking off and leading their way towards the pathway in the forest without having a clue where it would lead them to.

"The 'ass clowns', Unk?" asked EJ, confused and looking at Wicks as if he personally held the answers to not only that, but all of the world's questions.

They all had their respective bikes started now, old German TS motorbikes from so long ago, the rust had rust growing on it. Wicks looked to EJ seriously, saying, "Yea, you know, the 'ass clowns' who run the country, Neph! We gotta get some electric cars and shit, and eat jalapeños to save the planet from global warming!" Wicks then took off, popping a wheelie after Shelby.

"Electric cars and jalapeños?" asked EJ to Wicks back, before looking over to Serge, then Celiane, who shrugged her shoulders and held onto Serge as he took off, leaving EJ to bring up the rear. "Is everybody going crazy around here, or what?" he asked himself, looking back at the completely destroyed former mansion, and finally twisting the throttle on his dirt bike, following behind Celiane, making sure to do his part to get her home, safe and sound.

Celiane held on for dear life as they rode through the woods on a path that, at some places, just got a bit too close for comfort on a four-wheeler, but they went on for well over an hour and made it quite a few miles away, escaping the FAR. They soon landed on a dirt road that led them to another dirt road at a T-section. After Shelby's GPS led them in the right direction, they came to a city where Serge quickly stole a van and they immediately headed back over to Cien Fuegos.

Once they were back at the hut with a safe Marta and Catalina, their plan was to send Celiane with Serge to steal a boat at BAHIA DE CIEN FUEGOS, and to be waiting for them to get the girls back, take care of Chacho, Tip and Sweets-if he was even still alive-but then, Celiane screamed bloody murder to veto that idea.

Celiane is insistent that she not only rescue the girls with them, but also she wanted and needed to confront her captors and abusers, if only to show them that she fought the good fight and prove to them that she had now won. And she then also needed to see their eyes as their souls left their bodies after their lives were taken from them. She needed to know that they would not ever be able to hurt anybody else. Would never pimp another girl into sexual slavery. She needs closure, and tonight, she will see it through. She will not stop until she gets her closure, and her desired results. She has continuously proved herself to be a fighter and a survivor, and she does so again now.

Chapter Thirty

Tip sat at her desk as she spoke on the phone to the *Policia* Captain, trying to get back what she felt rightfully belonged to her. Chacho sat across from her in the visitor's chair worrying. After all they had been through and all the drama that had come with this Celiane girl in the first place, he couldn't for the life of him, figure out why Tip was still talking about paying to get her back! No girl in the world was worth all of the trouble she had caused, or all of the money that she had cost them. He just wanted to forget about Celiane, to finish paying off Manera's family and then to move on to bigger and better things. Money making things, like the OnlyFans and webcam sessions, since he was excited that they had finally been able to come up on the passwords to those accounts. He couldn't wait to put those to use, so why was she steady pressing this stupid shit? he wondered.

"What the fuck do you-" started Tip, before the person on the other end of the phone had obviously interrupted her unceremoniously. She sat listening to the voice on the other end of the phone as incredulity began to spread all across her face. A rare event all in itself.

"Are you fucking serious right now?" she asked. "You're talking about that pretty little niece of his that works at the *Policlinico* that ... Jesus ... "

Chacho sat reeling at the fact that for once, in all the time he had known her, Tip was actually speechless, her face beginning to betray her building anxiety at whatever information that she was being given in response to their inquiries into getting their girl back. Whatever it was, it didn't look good, of that, he was sure.

A shocked look on her face, Tip slowly put the phone down on her desk. She opened her mouth as she looked to Chacho, but the words just wouldn't come. She closed her mouth and looked to the ceiling, wheels turned 100 MPH, actually confused.

"What? What did they say?" asked Chacho, completely stunned to see Tip's unsure and anxious reaction to the updates that she had just received.

"They're gone ... They're all gone ... "

"Who's gone? Tip! What the fuck is going on? What happ-" started Chacho, frantically trying to get to the bottom of things before being interrupted by gunshots close by. Extremely close by.

He looked over to the closed office door, then back to Tip, who was just starting to get up as he heard the door behind him kicked open. The sound of a big crash was made and then more gunfire could be heard down the hall. A raid.

Tip, in that same instant, her natural reflexes being much sharper than Chacho's, was pulling her Kimber out of her holster with her right hand-but was immediately stopped by a three round burst. The shots rang out just as Tip had the Kimber R-7 gripped in her right hand, and was bringing it up into a shooting position. The menacing 9mm Kimber flew from her hand as three bullets from Wicks' Kel-Tec RDB Defender hit her in her right shoulder, causing her to lose the use of her right hand, as well as the Kimber itself, which had gone flying away from her.

"Don't do that ... Tip, is it?" said Wicks, calmly walking slowly up to Chacho, who was still in a deep state of shock. He just froze. He could say or do nothing. His reaction was like molasses.

Wicks slowly got right up close to Chacho, placed his Kel-Tec assault rifle right up to his head and let another three round burst loose, blowing his brains out and onto the same wall where Sweets brains had been, less than 48 hours before. "That's from Este, out of Wynwood ... "

"Hey! What the fuck?! Come-on now, whoever the fuck you are, we can work this shit out! Don't get all violent! I can fix this and I'll compensate you for any inconvenience, just take it easy," said Tip, trying to regain control of the situation while hiding any fear or emotional tells. Ever the gangsta. Though she had long ago lost control of this situation and wouldn't be controlling it anytime soon with Wicks involved.

"Chacho was your ... boyfriend?" inquired Wicks. "Where did you find him at? Such a scumbag. I know him as a well-known Chomo, molesting little young girls all over South Florida. Do you plan on compensating all of those families of the abused little girls as well? Or on paying for therapy for those who now lost their normal childhoods and have been sentenced to a lifetime of pain and of mental anguish from the abuse they have suffered? They will never be able to heal, never have a normal life. He has taken that from them. Can you replace that?"

"I didn't-" started Tip.

263

"Know?" asked Wicks, interrupting her attempted justification. "Whether you knew or not, it doesn't matter to me, to those girls. Even if you didn't know you're still affiliated with him ..."

She wouldn't beg. Wicks could see and knew this much. He knew she is a gangsta at the end of the day and knew that she was a tough bitch, regardless of her choice in company. Wicks didn't care if she begged or not, he would not get off on her death either way. He is just a very focused individual. His mission was simple. They both knew this and had accepted as much. She, just hoping for a compromise, and he, for an ending. For justice. A street justice.

As Tip sat on the floor behind her desk bleeding all over the ground around her, Wicks kept his weapon trained center mass on her. Silence had taken over the whole compound and Wicks exhaled a breath of relief. They both knew by that point, that Wicks' team had taken out all of her security and off-duty Cuban *Policia* that helped to ward off any robbery attempts such as this one currently taking place. He had control and she knew and accepted this much. She couldn't stop it if she tried. Her fate was forever sealed. The only thing she didn't understand was, why she was still alive when he obviously had the upper hand.

"What now?" she asked, ready to die, yet still wanting an out.

"Now, we deal," said Shelby as she walked in, several disheveled young girls standing behind her in the doorway. Celiane was leading them all in, vengeance shining brightly in her determined eyes.

"Now, you have a chance to live ... or ... you can die," said Shelby as she looked from Wicks, still pointing his nasty looking Kel-Tec towards Tip, and making direct eye contact with this infamous brothel madam. Or Pimp. Whatever was a more accurate description of her. It made no difference to any of them. Only her crimes did-her making victims out of these young girls mattered, and that was all.

"Tip, we gotta tax ya ... " added Wicks being nonchalant, yet very serious as well. "Let's say, ten bands per girl, that will help compensate them for all of the hardship and help pay for their schooling. Plus our fee. Plus making us come all the way over to this communist hell ... let's call it an even $200,000 and we let you live."

"Two hundred fucking-"

"Or ... we can just kill you now," interrupted Shelby as she ejected her half-empty magazine from her Colt AR-15 platform rifle and replaced it with a fresh 30 round mag, then charging one into the chamber.

"Jesus fucking-alright! Fucking deal. Bitcoin okay? I don't have that kind of cash just laying around here, ya know?" answered Tip.

"Bitcoin is fine. Shelby? Ladies?" said Wicks, indicating to all of the small American girls who were gathering behind Shelby in the hallway. "Will you and Ty escort the girls over to our vehicle and I'll handle our transaction with Tip?"

"C'mon, girls. Let's get y'all home to your families," Shelby said, leading the girls away.

Celiane refused, opting to stay instead.

As the rest of them left, Wicks went over to Tip, patted her down, and then got her laptop off of the desk, gently handing it to her, as she lie on the dirty floor behind the desk.

He pulled up the correct app on his phone, allowing her to type in his information as she brought up her own Bitcoin account and performed the transaction.

"You know I'll be looking for you to get this back, right?" said Tip, smiling.

"I know ... " answered Wicks, as he followed the transaction on his own account on his phone app.

PING!

His phone sounded off, letting him know that the transaction was complete and that the girls' money had been transferred. Celiane then approached, looking expectedly to Wicks.

"Okay, good," said Wicks. "Now, to complete our business, where is this 'Sweets' at?"

Tip laughed as she glanced at the bloody wall. "That was his brains on the wall before Chacho's. I guess we can say they were 'like-minded' ! Hahahaha!" said Tip, continuing on in her evil laughter, feeling safe in her own mortality after the transaction had been completed.

Wicks was unmoved, but he couldn't resist a retort. As Celiane turned away, knowing what was coming, Wicks really shared her mindset about Chacho and Sweets.

"Then I guess you are all of 'one mind'! So, if you want your money back that I took, get it from them when you get down there to hell and-" he started saying.

"Wait! Wha! But you said that-" started Tip, starting to panic and interrupting him in shock.

Wicks was already moving toward her as she is laying on the floor, his mind already made up and his rough aggressiveness showing his decision without even beating around the bush. Wicks allowed his Kel-Tec Defender to fall from his hands, letting it hang from its shoulder strap as he picked up Tip's Kimber R-7 and moved right into her personal space.

He grabbed a handful of her dirty blonde hair, wrapping it around his clenched left fist, and quickly snatched her up to her feet, lifting her by her hair.

"I fucking-" she started, but Wicks pistol-whipped her in the mouth, shattering her jaw and shutting her up once and for all.

Wicks yanked her over and mushed her face into the bloody wall covered in skull and brain fragments. Letting go of her hair, he placed the Kimber under her broken jaw, looking into her eyes before he pulled the required four pounds of pressure on the R-7's trigger, watching as this evil gangsta's thinking cap was blown off. Tip's own brains, blood and skull fragments were immediately sprayed all over the same wall that Sweets and Chacho's lives had both been ended on, their brains co-mingling together in death, just as they had in life, literally becoming of one mind, as Wicks had said before taking her life.

"Now all you like-minded muthafuckas can start a think tank together ... " said Wicks to their dead bodies, trailing off while brains were trailing down the wall, all of their evil thoughts stuck together forever.

"I don't know-give it some thought," he added, smiling finally, his mouth full of gold slugs gleaming brightly, looking out of place in the gruesome scene, his sarcastically macabre sense of humor finally coming to surface now that it was all over and Celiane was safe-soon to be home where she belongs: with her family.

Epilogue

Hinc illae lacrimae (Latin):

Hence those tears

"Your Honor, with all due respect, I object to this ruling! Spontaneous utterance rules permit this type of hearsay evidence for particularly this exact instance and-" started the prosecutor, after just hearing the defendant's suppression hearing and Motion in *Limini* being granted and all hearsay evidence being excluded from being used in his triple homicide case trial.

"Mr. Lawson! Are you making a mockery of this Court's ruling? Because if you are, I will not have it! You have no witnesses, and as your office-or the Sheriff's Office seem to have lost the murder weapon, and because you can't charge Mr. Jean with being at the scene ... " said Judge Richard Winnet, leaving the rest unsaid, the clear interpretation clear for everyone present.

"Your Honor, we can charge him with conspiracy to commit the one murder, resulting in the other two-"

"Charge away, counselor. I have no say in what the State of Florida wishes to charge Mr. Jean with, but it had better have merit. You had better present a whole lot more than what you've got at the preliminary hearing, because this court will tolerate no frivolous charging documents, nor will it permit a vindictive prosecution in its venue. In fact, it is this Court's recommendation that no charges are further pursued against Mr. Jean.. At least until you have some actual evidence, tying him to an actual crime. Is that understood, Mr. Lawson?"

"Yes, Your Honor," said the chastised prosecutor, thoroughly upset and disappointed, but not enough so to risk the wrath of the Court and being held in contempt of court.

"Okay, good. Now, Mr. Kline? Does the defense have a motion for the Court?" asked the Judge, almost rhetorically, since everyone in the courtroom knew what was coming next.

Apparently, there was someone who especially knew what was coming next, because it was at this juncture in time that she chose to stand up and prepared to walk out. The odd thing was that, all eyes were immediately drawn to her. She had that kind of look.. Classy, yet incredibly sexy. Nearly 6 feet in heels with big double D-Cup breasts accentuated by the tailored red Gucci pant suit, she is simply stunning. Quite beautiful even. A look passes between her and the tattoo-faced man at the defense table with the yellow dreads. Then, in a flash of beautiful hair, oblivious to the attention, she is gone.

"Yes, Your Honor. Mr. Jean would like to move to dismiss these charges for lack of prosecutorial evidence and the 180 day speedy trial date being up in two days. We move for Josue Jean to be immediately released, and for compensation for attorney's fees. Thank you, Your Honor," said the defense lawyer, Charles Kline.

"Case number 10-80159 is dismissed. Josue Jean is to be released from custody, but your last motion for attorney's fees is denied, Mr. Kline. I believe that Mr. Jean can pay his own private lawyer, don't you? Nice try though .... "

"Thank you, Your Honor."

"Case number 10-80159 is closed, court is adjured," finished the Judge.

Claps, as well as a few cries of joy in the open courtroom were heard. One in particular was Celiane, having been returned from the land of the dead, and grateful for it, as she jumped over the wooden divider and into her father's arms, after the sheriff deputies had just released him from his handcuffs to hug his daughter. There were smiles all around the courtroom on Attorney Kline-and Wicks'-side of the courtroom, but the prosecutor's side was absolutely livid. The State Attorney's Office had considered this kind of case a 'slam dunk', so this was not only a surprise, but it was a real embarrassment on the law enforcement community and the judicial side as well. Especially for the fact about them losing the evidence.

For some strange reason, all of the witnesses from a well known jack shack, Relax, had all disappeared or decided that they couldn't identify Josue as the killer at the scene. Others' statements had changed. To make matters even worse for the prosecution, either the State Attorney's Office, or the Palm Beach County Sheriff's Office, had lost the infamous Saturday Night Special .38 snubnose revolver that had allegedly been the gun that fired the bullets that killed Tree. This was, of course, before they could be matched by ballistic testing. The former was blaming the latter for the loss of evidence this crucial in a triple homicide, and vice versa.

271

It looked bad for both of the agencies. Nobody wanted to take the blame.

It had either been a stroke of luck for Celiane and her father, or by a determined and intricate plan and grand design on Wicks' behalf, that this crucial evidence had turned up missing. It had never made it from the forensics department to ballistics, where it needed to be formally tested to match the bullets with those that had been pulled out of Tree's body by the Medical Examiner. Again, one department blaming the other department for the loss of evidence. Both departments looking stupid and incompetent.

The really funny thing about it that nobody seemed to have figured out or even considered, is that the Palm Beach County Sheriff's evidence room officer, Oscar Rojas, was a big and compulsive gambler. Not only did he play poker and blackjack at the Palm Beach Kennel Club's gambling tables and the Palm Beach Princess Casino cruise ship, he also owed a lot of money and was well-known in some of the Gambini Family's speak-easy gambling houses. These are run by Gambini family operators, to whom someone with clout could make a call to. Someone like Lexi Gambini-Lexi Marley. The call was made, evidence 'lost', and Oscar Rojas' debts were cleared.

As Wicks' new boss, Mr. Kline, and Celiane's whole family celebrated being reunited with Josue. None of them noticed Wicks take out his phone after feeling its vibration alert ... None of them read the message that was from Lexi Marley that said 'you owe me one .... ' none of them noticed all of Wicks 20 gold teeth shining in what passes as a smile for Wicks. And of course, none of them noticed what he texted her back, "Don't make it an easy one, I love a challenge ... "

None of them noticed anything beyond each other. Family. None of them noticed because they are all too happy with what they have in front of them. A complete and happy family. United as one. Together. And they would never again lose sight of that or allow anything to come between them. Never again would they be victims. Happiness is a fight to the death, and they had all won on this happy day. They would always be grateful to Wicks and Shelby. They would never forget their blessings, and they would always cherish their family. Family would always come first for them. Always. As it should ...

About the Author

Taboo, or Brian Micko Yeary, is a Federal Prisoner who has been sentenced to die in prison for non-violent, victimless gun and drug possessions charges. Being an advocate for Criminal Justice Reform and while waiting for retroactivity to apply the First Step Act to his stacked 924(c) sentences, Taboo started FREE TABOO PUBLISHING, LLC to bring attention not only to his own situation, but to also help to publish other talented authors and poets who are also Victims of Justice incarcerated in this criminal INjustice system.

Sentenced to 91 years for a draconian 924(c) sentencing enhancement that has since been corrected by Congress, Taboo still sits under this unfair and ridiculous sentence. Convinced by Tom Cotton of Arkansas, Congress decided that the 924(c) law is only unfair to those who were sentenced AFTER 2018 and not those who are actually still suffering right now from the unfairness of it, so they withheld retroactivity from older cases sentenced before the First Step Act.

Most convicts in Taboo's position would become a product of their environment in a Maximum Security Penitentiary overrun by gangs and violence, but this author instead persevered and established FREE TABOO PUBLISHING in April 2022 and introduced his debut novel, "*A Victim of Justice*" shortly thereafter. He has two new authors to introduce and a trilogy of his own coming out soon. He lives in Lee County US Penitentiary with no cats, dogs, yet a lot of hope in Congress to pass legislation for retroactivity and equality in sentencing reform.